A Dead Ringer...

I was the only one inside when the phone rang.

Probably the Welcome Wagon Lady, I thought. I went to the kitchen and picked up the receiver. "Hello?"

There was the sound of a bell ringing, like the kind of bell a little kid would have mounted on a bicycle handle. *Brring bring! Brring bring!*

"Hello," I said in my most pleasant singsong.

The tinny bell rang again.

"Last chance," I warned, still trying to sound friendly.

The bell stopped and I was about to hang up when a little voice said, "Help me."

"What?" It sounded like a kid, probably a little girl.

"Please." Several seconds. "Help me."

"Are you home alone?" I asked.

The damn bicycle bell *brring*ed again.

Danny and Dad walked into the kitchen.

"Not fair!" Danny squealed. "Here we are working our butts off, and Brenda's on the phone already."

Dad was shaking his head. "The phone doesn't work, honey. It won't be hooked up till Monday."

BEING
DEAD

BEING DEAD

VIVIAN VANDE VELDE

Magic Carpet Books • Harcourt, Inc.

ORLANDO   AUSTIN   NEW YORK   SAN DIEGO   TORONTO   LONDON

www.HarcourtBooks.com

First Magic Carpet Books edition 2003

Magic Carpet Books is a trademark of Harcourt, Inc.,
registered in the United States of America and/or other jurisdictions.

The Library of Congress has cataloged the hardcover edition as follows:
Vande Velde, Vivian.
Being dead: stories/by Vivian Vande Velde.
p. cm.
Summary: Seven supernatural stories, all having something to do with death.
1. Supernatural—Juvenile fiction.   2. Children's stories, American.
[1. Supernatural—Fiction.   2. Horror stories.   3. Short stories.]   I. Title.
PZ7.V2773Be   2001
[Fic]—dc21   00-12996
ISBN 0-15-216320-4
ISBN 0-15-204912-6 pb

Text set in Electra
Designed by Cathy Riggs

C E G H F D

Printed in the United States of America

CONTENTS

Drop by Drop   1

Dancing with Marjorie's Ghost   61

Shadow Brother   69

The Ghost   109

For Love of Him   117

October Chill   135

Being Dead   175

BEING
DEAD

Drop by Drop

The first thing I remember about Saturday was I had a headache that felt as though tiny aliens were trying to chew their way out of my head through my left eyeball, and my brother, Danny, was being obnoxious. I mean, I know I'd gotten up earlier, because there I was, dressed and in the car, but mercifully I had no memory of that. For me the day started in the car.

Danny's earphones leaked a tinny stream of rap. The beat was as effective on my headache as someone smacking the side of my head with a Ping-Pong paddle. At the same time, he was stabbing at the keys of some handheld electronic game that kept beeping and playing its own annoying little tune every time he scored. And then he'd crow, "Yes!" as though he were winning at something worthwhile.

In the front seat Mom had cranked up her own music to drown him out. Probably as a concession to us, she hadn't put in one of her opera tapes, but *The Little Mermaid* wasn't much better. There's nothing like Sebastian the crab howling "Under the Sea" to start off your morning right.

Dad was smart enough to be driving the rented U-Haul without us.

Danny had his feet crossed up on the seat, so that his knee kept jabbing me in the side. And his stack of coloring books and comic books and snack bags had tipped over onto me, too.

Ten o'clock in the morning, and the car's air-conditioning was already losing its battle with the August heat.

I shoved Danny and he shoved back.

"Mom," I complained, "Danny's crowding me."

"Ma," chimed in Danny, "Brenda didn't brush her teeth this morning, and she's breathing morning breath all over me."

"Stop fighting." Mom never even looked back to see how much of the seat Danny was taking. "We're almost there." If she had been a concerned parent, she would have let me sit up front instead of subjecting me to Danny. But the front seat was reserved for transporting plants that she had to keep an eye on so they wouldn't tip. It's a sad state of affairs when a coleus takes precedence over a family's firstborn child. Then again, if my mother or father were concerned parents, we wouldn't be moving in the first place.

"How close is 'almost there'?" I asked.

"Half an hour till our exit, then another forty minutes to the house."

An hour and ten minutes is *not* almost there. It barely qualified as halfway there.

"I have a headache, and I think I'm getting carsick."

"Oh, Brenda," Mom said, "you don't get carsick."

Easy for her to say.

Danny said, "She went out drinking with her friends, and now she's hungover. That's why her eyes are all red. Either that, or she's turning into a vampire."

I curled my lip at him in a snarl. "If I ever *did* become a vampire, I know who my first victim would be."

Mom told him, "Sixteen is too young to go out drinking. And Brenda's friends are too nice to be vampires."

"Oh," Danny said innocently, "then maybe it's just her regular PMS."

Midget pervert, I mouthed at him. I certainly wasn't going to admit to either of them that I'd cried myself to sleep the night before. I found my sunglasses and put them on. To my mother I could have said, *I don't have any friends; not anymore, thank you very much.* But I knew what she would say: *Then make some new ones.* Like moving when you're sixteen is the same as moving when you're eleven.

My parents were ruining my life, and they wanted me to consider it an adventure.

A half hour later my dad, in the U-Haul ahead of us, signaled to get off the Thruway. We followed him into a little town.

Was this the fabled promised land of Westport, New York?

Apparently not. We drove straight through and out again.

Into a smaller town.

And out the far end of that place, too.

We drove past a gas station (cleverly named GAS) and a restaurant (mercifully *not* called EATS). Did a gas station and a restaurant qualify as yet another town? (Welcome to the town of GAS. Population: two fully qualified mechanics and one short-order cook.) Mostly we drove past lots and lots of fields. It was hard to believe this area had enough people to support a community college, but that was where my parents were going to work—Westport CC—my father teaching business, my mother computer science. The other courses were probably things like Introduction to the Digestive System of the Cow 101, and Goat Parasitology 203, and Advanced Tractor Repair. What were my parents thinking, bringing us out into the wilderness like this? We had to be hours away from the nearest mall.

Ahead of us the van's left-turn blinker began to flash.

"Here we are," Mom announced.

"Oh, wow," I said. "A paved road and everything."

The house itself was certainly bigger than anything we could have afforded in Buffalo, and it had a great expanse of yard, which I could have appreciated more if I hadn't suspected that *I* would be the one responsible for mowing it.

To make up for the road being paved, the driveway was not.

Dad got out of the moving van. He had a big Christmas-morning grin on his face. "What do you think?" he asked proudly.

What did I think?

How can you trust any neighborhood where the houses are so far apart you practically *have* to get into the car and drive to visit your next-door neighbor?

"Do we have running water?" I asked.

"Ay-yup," Dad said, trying for some kind of accent. "And I hear tell in the next year or so we may even be getting some of that newfangled electricity stuff."

There *were* poles, so I guessed he was joking. My headache was going away, but my father's sense of humor could bring it right back again.

"Well, I think it's cool," Danny said. Sometimes Danny waits to hear my opinion on things just so that he can say the opposite. "How much of this is ours?"

"Two acres." Mom pointed to the left. "From just after that speed limit sign"—she indicated to the right—"to that line of poplars over there. The backyard goes as far back as those other trees."

"That's not enough land to farm," Danny said.

"Thank God," I muttered in relief that my parents couldn't get ideas and get carried away with themselves.

Mom ignored me. "There's a patch for a vegetable garden," she told Danny.

Not being big on vegetables, unless you count french fries, Danny shrugged. "No animals?"

"There's a pond," Dad said.

That brightened Danny back up. "For swimming?"

Dad shook his head. "No, it's only a little bit bigger than that wading pool you had a couple years back. It's for fish."

"Who has to take care of them?" I demanded suspiciously.

"They take care of themselves," Dad assured me.

Uh-huh. So does our self-cleaning oven, in theory.

My parents were real eager for us to see our rooms, so I barely glimpsed the living room before we went up the stairs. My room was first. The walls were white, but the ceiling was a deep midnight blue, and whoever had this room before me had stuck up glow-in-the-dark stars.

My father looked at me expectantly.

What can I say? Five years ago I would have loved it.

8

"Or," Mom offered, "your father can scrape the stars off and repaint whatever color you want."

"No," I said. "It's fine. Really." I tried to make my voice sound enthusiastic.

Danny, little opportunist that he is, said, "If she doesn't want it, I'll take it."

Mom said, "This *is* the biggest bedroom after ours, and it has the walk-in closet. But if you'd like to see the other rooms..."

A walk-in closet *was* nice.

"No, this is fine," I mumbled.

There was also a bow window that had a seat and overlooked the backyard with its trees and bushes and the pond my parents had told us about.

My parents got the master bedroom, which had a little alcove that Mom called a reading nook. Danny got the room that had a lot of built-in shelves, which was good for him because Danny has all sorts of collections: comic books, action figures, baseball cards, model race cars, stones and seashells from places we've visited. Basically anything that doesn't move, Danny collects. (Things that move, too—but if Mom catches him, she makes him release them.) There was a fourth bedroom that Mom said would be the combination spare bedroom/computer room/sewing room.

As we walked back downstairs Dad put his arm around my shoulders. "I thought you'd like that ceiling," he said.

"It's fine," I told him.

"I can paint it."

I shook my head. It would take about five coats of paint before that blue wouldn't show through. What difference did it make, anyway? Here we were, stuck out in the country. It wasn't like I was ever going to make any friends that I could invite over. What would we talk about? Chicken diseases? Country and Western singers? Our 4-H projects? My life was on hold until I went to college, which I knew would be back in Buffalo, whatever I decided to major in. That was something we had pledged to last night, Traci and Tina and Jennie and me: I'd go back to Buffalo, and they wouldn't leave. We'd be back together in two years. You can survive two years of just about anything if you have a goal.

So we began to move into our new house, box by box by box by box.

I was the only one inside when the phone rang.

Probably the Welcome Wagon lady, I thought—the Welcome Wagon striking me as a very rustic concept. She probably wanted to find out when she should drop off her homemade jams, pigs' feet, and pickle preserves. I went to the kitchen and picked up the receiver. "Hello?"

There was the sound of a bell ringing, like the kind of bell a little kid would have mounted on a bicycle handle. *Brrring bring! Brrring bring!*

"Hello," I said in my most pleasant singsong.

The tinny bell rang again.

"Last chance," I warned, still trying to sound friendly. "Hello." This was probably country people's idea of a prank call.

The bell stopped and I was about to hang up when a little voice said, "Help me."

"What?" It sounded like a kid, probably a little girl, probably about seven or eight.

"Please." Several seconds. "Help me."

Most likely it was a prank, I told myself. Even though the voice sounded frightened, that could be faked. But who would know this number?

Aware I was no doubt showing myself as the gullible city girl to the local fun-loving yokels, I said, "Who are you trying to reach?"

"You," the voice said, half catching on a sigh or a gulp for air.

If this was a prank—and I knew from personal experience that for every voice you hear in a prank call, there are at least two other kids ready to explode from suppressed laughter—if they were pranksters, they were good: just the right amount of scared and pathetic without being overdone.

"Are you home alone?" I asked.

The damn bicycle bell *brrring*ed again.

Danny and Dad walked into the kitchen.

"Not fair!" Danny squealed. "Here we are working our butts off, and Brenda's on the phone already."

"The phone doesn't work, honey," Dad told me.

"It rang," I explained. "There's some little kid." Into the phone, I asked, "Are you still there?"

No answer, and Dad was shaking his head. "It won't be hooked up till Monday. Someone from the phone company has to check the wires."

"But maybe it's the old number," I said—that would explain, if the child on the other end was trying to reach the people who used to live here—but whoever was on the line wasn't talking or *brrring*ing that bell or anything. Still, I hadn't heard a click as though she had hung up. "Hello? Hello?" I jiggled the phone cradle. Nothing; not even a dial tone. "It rang," I repeated.

"Wishful thinking," Danny said. "Or the first symptoms of dementia."

"Maybe crossed wires," Dad offered.

That would explain the bell, I guessed. I put the receiver back down. I hoped the little kid reached whoever she was trying to get.

Lunch was lemonade from powder, and sandwiches Mom had packed the night before. Under the best of circumstances, Mom is not an enthusiastic cook.

After lunch the plan was that Mom and Dad would

drive the U-Haul back to Buffalo to get the second load from our old house, and the second car. Danny and I were supposed to unpack the stuff for our own rooms.

"Don't worry about the kitchen and the bathroom closet," Mom told me. "I'll do that."

I shrugged. "I can at least start." It wasn't like I had anything else to do with my life for the next two years.

"I need to decide where things go," Mom said. "I can't make decisions this fast."

"Don't," I agreed with her. She was getting that frantic put-upon look she gets when she feels pressured by too many things needing to be done.

She looked around the kitchen. "You could clean out the cupboards. The rubber gloves and the cleaning supplies are in one of those two boxes."

Oh, boy. Cleaning.

"Why don't you stay?" I offered. "I can drive the Honda." That's the one they let me drive—when they let me drive.

But Mom shook her head. "I need to make sure the old place is presentable for the new people."

Heaven forbid that the strangers moving in should think poorly of us because of Mom's housekeeping skills.

"Don't forget to keep an eye on the water-bed hose," Dad reminded me.

Danny and I waved good-bye, then set to organizing our rooms.

With my walk-in closet I had so much room that it didn't take me long to get my stuff settled. And I couldn't make my bed until it finished filling.

Dad had bought an adapter so that the hose could be hooked up to the kitchen tap, filling the mattress real slowly with warm water so that I'd be able to sleep in my bed that night. We'd learned that trick when I'd first gotten the bed—when the heater that's under the mattress took about two days to heat up the water that came from the outside spigot.

No leaks, and Dad had it going so slowly I probably wouldn't have to turn it off until he and Mom got back. I definitely had a couple hours to spare, so I didn't have to start in on those cupboards this very minute.

"I'm going outside," I yelled to Danny.

"Lucky," he complained. Luck had nothing to do with it—if he didn't have so much junk, he'd be through, too.

I wanted to see the little backyard pond. I wondered if the old people had left the fish, or if we'd have to get our own. Was that the kind of thing covered by a purchase agreement? I mean, if you had a dog when you were moving, you wouldn't expect to have to leave the dog along with the doorknobs and the wallpaper.

As I walked out into the backyard, I could hear the faint *brrring bring* of a bicycle bell. I wondered if it was the same kid who had called, and if she lived next door, and if she'd solved her problem, whatever it was. But I couldn't see the house next door—too much yard, too many trees between. Probably all the kids out here had bicycle bells—to warn the cows away. This particular kid using this particular bell kept going and going. That would grow old fast.

When I got to the pond, it was, as Dad had said, about the size of a small wading pool. But it wasn't cheesy. It was surrounded by plants and had what I figured was probably the setup for a miniature waterfall to cascade down artfully placed rocks. It didn't exactly look natural, but it wasn't like something you'd see in Wal-Mart, either. The waterfall wasn't going, and I realized there had to be some sort of pump to circulate the water. Then it came to me: That would be the switch in the kitchen, the one with the little bit of masking tape over it that said PUMP. That was a relief. When I had seen that word *pump,* I had gotten an immediate mental picture of one of those hand pumps out in the front yard that you see in Westerns, the kind the farm wife in her apron stands next to as she tells the boys, "Time to stop herdin' them cattle and wash up afore supper."

The whole setup was pretty. Not as pretty as my friend Jennie's rose garden, but pretty in a wildflower kind of way.

It was hard to tell if there were any fish. There were lots of rocks and water plants, both in and around the pond, and I was trying not to trample anything.

Something splashed, though I wasn't quick enough to see what. So there *were* fish. Or frogs. That was kind of neat.

Another splash, in the same area as before. I still couldn't see anything. I waited where I was, hoping that if I stayed long enough I'd see something.

The third splash came from exactly where the previous two had. All right. Apparently if I was to see anything, I was going to have to move closer. I stepped on some of the decorative rocks between the plants at the edge of the water.

Yet another splash. This time I caught a glimpse of something light colored. One of those fat pale goldfish, maybe, jumping into the air? Was it trying to catch something? Or was *it* caught on something and trying to wriggle loose? I hoped I wouldn't need to administer first aid to a fish.

I put one knee down on a rock and leaned over the murky water. I couldn't make out the bottom, couldn't make out any movement. "I bet you just waited for me to get here before you'd move," I whispered to the fish. It was only when I heard my own voice that I was aware the bicycle bell had finally stopped.

The water in front of me rippled, so I had fair warning that the fish was moving. I waited for it to come to the surface....

Except it wasn't a fish that flopped in the water—it was a hand.

I sat back with a startled yelp.

The hand clawed at the air—I could distinctly see the fingers—then it disappeared back under the water.

Jeez! Some kid must have fallen in and was drowning right there in front of me. "Hold on!" I yelled at the kid in the pond, even though there was no way a kid entirely underwater could hear me. I scrambled to my feet and waded in.

And found that the pond was only a foot and a half at its deepest.

How could any kid bigger than a baby drown in a foot and a half of water?

And there was no kid.

There I was stomping around on all those delicate little water plants—and no kid. Nothing that looked at all like a human hand. Whatever had been flopping in the water wasn't flopping anymore.

I don't want to do this; I don't want to do this, I told myself. But I had to, just in case. I forced myself to reach down with my hand, to feel in the dark water, to touch the mucky, slippery bottom.

I jerked back. Was that hair? Had I just touched someone's hair?

Or was it those wispy plant tendrils?

Clamping my teeth together to keep them from chattering, I once more reached into the cold water. Tendrils brushed my fingers, just tendrils.

I took a step forward to check that last corner of the pond.

Nothing.

Except that the pump suddenly turned on, which had to mean Danny was in the kitchen, watching me be a fool.

Setup, I thought. There might not have been a drowning kid in the pool before, but let me get my hands on Danny....

I clambered out of the pond, squashing more of the plants and upsetting a little tower of rocks.

Gee, I thought sarcastically, *maybe Mom and Dad won't notice.*

I walked back to the house, my sneakers squishing rudely with each step.

No sign of Danny. Smart boy. *But he can't have found a good enough hiding place*, I told myself.

Going upstairs I tripped over the hose to my water bed, even though I thought I wasn't stepping anywhere near it. The way things were going, I knew I'd better detour into my room to make sure I hadn't yanked the hose loose.

That wasn't the surprise I found in my bedroom.

The surprise was that the double doors to the closet were open and all my clothes were on the floor.

"Danny!" I yelled in fury.

"What?" he called from his room. That was not what I'd expected.

Still, "Get in here," I shouted.

"I'm busy."

I stomped down the hall to his room.

He looked up from arranging his action figures on one of his shelves and obviously took in that my shorts were wet and muddy. As though he hadn't already seen, he demanded, "What happened to you?"

"What happened to my room?"

The fact that Danny didn't have a snappy comeback, that he waited to hear what I was going to say, made his innocence more credible.

"Did you or did you not knock my clothes on the floor?" I asked.

"I did not," he said.

"And did you or did you not have a nasty little surprise for me in the pond, and then you turned on the pump once you had tricked me into going in?"

"You were in the pond?" he asked. "With all the, like, fish poop and frog slime?" For a boy Danny could be awfully prissy. When he saw that I was still waiting for an answer, he added, "I never left my room."

And whatever I'd seen in the pond, on second, rational thought, wasn't anything Danny could have had anything to do with—he'd been helping tote stuff indoors from the car and the truck, then he'd been arranging his room the whole while since. He'd had no time to set up a joke.

I would have preferred a Danny joke to just about any other explanation I could think of.

It had probably been a sick or mutant frog, I tried to convince myself, or some exotic fish. If there could be bottlenose dolphins and hammerhead sharks, who was I to say there was no such species as a finger-finned something-or-other? I hadn't seen what I thought I'd seen, I told myself.

And I kept telling it to myself all the while I picked my clothes up off the floor of the closet. This time I made sure the clothes were securely on the hangers, and the hangers were properly hooked on the bar. And the fact that some of the clothes were damp only meant that I should have changed out of my wet shorts before starting.

I hadn't made up my mind if I was going to tell my parents about the weirdness of the afternoon—the big problem being *what* I could tell them—when they came home with the second vanful of stuff. It was nine o'clock in the evening.

Mom walked in complaining about the Honda. "Brenda," she asked, "did you notice when you were driving last night that it had a tendency to pull to the right?"

Hungry, and hot and tired from scrubbing the grease off the kitchen cabinet doors and from peeling off the Con-Tact paper that the shelves were lined with—Con-Tact paper that came off in one-inch strips—I demanded,

"How come you immediately assume I did something to break the car?"

Hungry and hot and tired herself, Mom snapped, "I'm not accusing you of breaking the car. I'm asking if you noticed that the car was pulling to the right."

"No," I said.

I didn't add that I had been too miserable about seeing my friends for the last time to notice much of anything. Well, I had run off the pavement, then back on, but surely cars aren't *that* delicate.

Dad said, "It probably just needs to be aligned. I'll make an appointment next week."

No doubt ticked off by my tone, Mom muttered, "It didn't need to be aligned yesterday morning when *I* drove it." To my father she added, "She isn't even supposed to drive at night."

Here we go again, I thought.

Dad, the peacemaker, said, "It's probably been out of alignment since this spring, when there were all those potholes. You just noticed it today because the car was riding low from all the stuff packed in it." Then he added—his usual complaint—"This family has too much stuff. Come on, let's unload, then we'll go out for pizza. We've got all of tomorrow to finish unpacking."

"Think Westport has a pizza place?" I scoffed, not willing to make peace that easily.

"No," Mom said, "I think you'll have to hunt down

some elk all by yourself, shoot it, skin it, and cook it over an open fire, because we've moved to Westport just to torment you."

And she tells *me* not to be sarcastic.

By the time we got back and had our showers, I wasn't in bed until after 1:00 A.M. I figured I'd be asleep in ten seconds. The last night in our old house, Dad had already drained my water bed, and I had to sleep on the couch. So, even if I hadn't gotten in at three—which was about two and a half hours later than I'd admitted to when my parents asked—I wouldn't have had a good night's sleep. But now here I was, exhausted from a long day's work, in my own cozy water bed, and I started to drift off right away.

I was so far gone I wasn't alarmed when I felt the mattress jiggle under me. *Traci's cat,* I thought muzzily. Then, right as I was about to drop off totally, I thought, *I'm not at Traci's house.*

I came awake enough to open my eyes and see that there wasn't anything sitting at the foot of the bed. I closed my eyes.

Something moved.

I sat up and turned on the light.

The light revealed . . . nothing.

The mattress sloshed around from my movement. *Just*

an air pocket, I reasoned. And by causing the mattress to slosh, I would have broken it up.

I turned the light off and settled down again. The water bed stopped moving.

Then started again.

A snake or a mouse had gotten in between the covers—I *knew* it.

I jumped up and yanked the top sheet down. Nothing. I pulled off the under sheet. Then the mattress pad. Nothing. Gingerly I poked with my toe at the comforter, which had fallen to the floor from where I keep it folded across the foot of the bed. I saw nothing. Which didn't guarantee that there was nothing there.

It wasn't bad enough my parents had to tear me away from my school and my friends to plunk me down in the middle of Green Acres? They had to buy a house that was crawling with vermin?

Reluctantly I picked up a corner of the comforter, sure that something was just waiting to run up my arm.

Nothing did.

"And don't come back," I muttered.

I shook out the sheets, just to be sure, then remade the bed. I switched off the light and climbed back into bed. Well, *that* was nice and restful. Home sweet home. I closed my eyes.

Something moved.

All right, I'm sixteen years old and I wasn't currently on speaking terms with my mother—but I ran to get my parents, anyway.

They were still up, reading in bed.

"There's something in my bed!" I yelled.

"Is it Goldilocks?" my father asked.

Mom, even though we were mad at each other, gave him a dirty look and followed me into my room.

Silently, still not talking to me, Mom pulled the sheet back a bit more than it already was.

I told her, "I took all the covers off and I couldn't see anything, then when I got back in, I felt whatever-it-was moving again."

My father came in carrying the flyswatter.

"I'm not talking about a bug," I told him, aware that my voice was veering into shrillness. "Something big enough to make the mattress move."

My parents didn't say anything, but they stripped the bed, shaking out the sheets.

"I *did* that already," I said.

"Could something have gotten between the mattress and the frame?" Mom asked Dad.

"Something big enough to make the mattress move?" Dad sounded skeptical. And understandably so. Even to get the corners of the mattress pad around the mattress, you've got to wedge and jam. It was hard to believe anything living could fit in there.

Still, Dad looked. He worked his way all around the bed, peeling the edge of the heavy mattress back from the frame.

"I don't see anything, honey," he assured me.

"This place has rats," I complained.

"No, it doesn't," Mom said, which I guess meant we were talking again, even if she was disagreeing with me. "I'll get fresh sheets."

I'm sure they were convinced it was a spider.

Mom and I made up the bed with the clean sheets.

"How's that?" Dad asked as I climbed back in.

I was about to grudgingly admit it was fine, when I felt something move beneath me.

I shot out of bed. "It's in the mattress!" I yelped.

"There can't be anything in the mattress," Dad protested as I once more pulled the bedding off.

We stared at the bare mattress. It's a dark blue plastic, so of course you can't see in, but I was sure we'd see it bulging here and there as whatever was inside poked around.

But we didn't.

"There's something in there," I insisted.

"A rat could not live in a water-bed mattress," Dad said. "First of all, how would it get in? Second, how would it breathe?"

I was angry, even though he was right. "I don't know," I said. "It doesn't have to be a rat. I couldn't see *what* it was. I only felt it."

Dad rested his hands on the bed. He moved them around, pressing, to entice whatever was in there to move. Nothing did.

"It would have to be a fish," Mom said.

Dad gave her a wary look.

"To live in the water."

"How would a fish get in?" Dad asked.

How could anything get in? We all looked at the plug in the water bed—just big enough to accommodate the end of a hose.

"I was only trying to be helpful," Mom said. Obviously she was joking, trying to lighten the mood. But talk of fish reminded me of what I'd seen in the pond that afternoon. Except that hadn't been a fish—it was a hand. Standing there in my bedroom, knowing that there was something in my water-bed mattress, I admitted to myself what I had been denying all afternoon: That hadn't been any kind of exotic or mutant or tumored fish or frog I'd seen in the pond—it had been a hand, a living hand, in a spot that wasn't big enough or deep enough to accommodate the person that hand had to be attached to.

And if my parents were looking at me weirdly now, how would they look if I told them *that*?

"I'm not getting back in that bed," I told them.

"Brenda . . . ," Dad said reasonably.

"I'm sleeping on the couch." I picked up my pillow. Dad sighed. "We'll drain the bed. Not now"—he glanced at my alarm clock, which showed 1:30—"but we'll do it in the morning."

I knew he wouldn't find anything in the morning.

It wasn't bad enough my parents had to move to Green Acres. They had to buy a house that was haunted.

Whatever had been in my water bed didn't migrate to the couch.

That does not mean I slept well. The house creaked. Cars went by all night long—not a lot of them, but *all night long*. And the boxes stacked in the living room suddenly struck me as a good place for something scary to hide behind. Then, early, early, early in the morning— just as in countless Disney films—I heard a rooster crow. But guess what? They don't do it just once. And you know what else? People always talk about good, fresh country air, but I kept getting whiffs of something that was neither good nor fresh but definitely country.

Of course, the bedrooms have window air-conditioning units; besides, my parents' room faces the backyard and Danny goes to sleep with his radio on, so none of them were bothered by the road noise. Apparently they slept through the barnyard racket and were oblivious to the fact that the whole house could use a breath mint. They woke up with way too much energy and good cheer.

When I come in after people are asleep, everyone expects me to close the door gently and tiptoe my silent way to bed. You'd think *they'd* have the same consideration for *me* when they get up while *I'm* asleep.

I moaned loudly to show that they were disturbing me, but they were making too much racket in the kitchen to hear. When I got up to complain, Mom said, "The day's only going to get hotter. The morning is the best time to work."

"Central air would be nice," I pointed out.

"So would a condo in Palm Beach," Mom said.

Which I guess meant *Lots of luck*.

Dad asked me, "What do you think; do you still want me to drain the water bed?"

"I don't care." I knew he wouldn't find anything.

Dad looked relieved, but Mom asked, "If we don't drain it, will you sleep in your room tonight?"

"No," I admitted. "But I won't even if you *do* drain it."

"You can't sleep on the couch for the rest of your life," Dad said.

"Just until college."

"Drain it," Mom told Dad. She was probably figuring if I got hot enough in the living room I'd return to my room for the air conditioner.

We spent the morning unpacking and settling in. Dad was in charge of hooking up the TV, VCR, and stereo. Danny put our books in the bookshelves. Mom and I worked in the kitchen—me washing, her drying all the dishes that we'd had to wrap in newspaper to protect during the move. But after a while I ended up doing both washing *and* drying, because she was having trouble settling what should go where in the kitchen cupboards ("That's the glasses cabinet; no, wait, that's where we'll keep the mugs; no, wait..."), and as she kept changing her mind, I ran out of space in the dish drainer.

When the water was all out of my bed, the mattress lay pretty much flat. Mom poked at the wrinkles left in the plastic. "Whatever it was could have drained out with the water," she suggested, looking at the hose that Dad had dangling out the window. "Was anybody watching?"

It had taken almost four hours. Of course nobody had been watching.

Danny snickered. "I think her brain drained out."

I wasn't sure it hadn't.

By then we were done with the dish washing, and Dad hooked the hose back up to the kitchen sink to refill the mattress.

By midafternoon the important boxes were all unpacked and flattened for recycling. Dad moved the remaining boxes into the basement, from where we could gradually unpack them as we needed the stuff, or at least wait until Mom had one of her I-can't-stand-this-clutter fits. Not that anyplace besides the basement was at all cluttered, but she gets like that. With everything either put away or still in its box, the house was neater than our house in Buffalo had usually looked, and the rooms were bigger, so it would take a longer time of things not being picked up before the place would look messy. We had more room to spread out, too. There was the extra bedroom, where Mom had set up a guest bed that looked a lot more comfortable than the couch, and that's where the computers went, too: the Mac for serious work, the IBM for games. And there was a wraparound porch, so you could sit in your rocker and watch the neighbor across the street hold up traffic by driving his tractor down the road, or you could sit on the right side of the house and watch that neighbor rounding up his cows. I still hated it.

"Want to go into town and see what there is to see?" Mom asked.

Go into town. See what there is to see. They were already talking like hicks.

"Thanks all the same," I said. "I'm going to take a shower."

"You can take one when we get back," Dad said.

"Oh, boy, good suggestion," Danny said, holding his nose.

"Yeah?" I told him. "What makes you think anybody wants to smell you after you've been working all morning?"

"We can leave the windows down," Dad offered.

I shook my head. I was so sticky I couldn't stand myself.

Mom said, "We can wait. We could go *after* your shower."

"No, you catch all the highlights," I said, "and you make out a list of what I need to see."

After they left I changed my mind about the shower. Things had been weird enough with the pond and the water bed so that when I stepped into the shower and started to pull the curtain closed, I had a sudden vision of that scene in *Psycho* where Janet Leigh meets Mother Bates.

Options: Well, I could wait for my parents to come back home after I'd made such a fuss about needing a shower right away.

Or I could hose myself off in the driveway.

I opted for a bath instead. Not that I expected anyone to sneak up on me. But at least that way if someone *did*, I could hear him coming.

I put in an extra scoop of Mr. Bubble, so the bubbles were extravagantly close to overflowing, then decided to be entirely decadent and poured myself some wine. (The glasses had ended up in the cupboard to the left of the sink.) Sometimes my parents let me have half a glass of wine with dinner, but they would not have approved this, so I knew I would have to make sure the glass was washed and back in its place by the time they came back.

Standing next to the tub, I couldn't help myself: I stuck my foot in and pushed the bubbles around enough that I could be sure there was nothing besides the bubbles in there. *Brenda*, I told myself as I got in, *sometimes you can be such a baby.* But I still felt better for having checked.

I balanced the wine on the edge of the tub and was taking the "How Fashion Savvy Are You?" quiz in *Cosmo* and was feeling pretty savvy and downright sophisticated when I reached for the glass and felt something drip on my arm.

I was in a tub—of course things were drippy. I didn't even glance up from the page I was on. I took a sip from the glass, and only then, with my arm crossed in front of me, did I see a red spot on the back of my forearm.

Why am I not surprised that something is dripping rust in this old bathroom? I asked myself. But even as I thought it, I knew it wasn't rust. Rust is more orange. And the wine I had poured myself was blush, not nearly that red.

I looked up.

A little girl was standing there.

My heart felt as though it stopped for a second, then it began to thud. The wineglass dropped from my numb fingers into the bathwater.

I tried to jump to my feet, and my heel slipped before I'd gotten more than a couple inches up—so that I sat down heavily, smacking my butt and sloshing water over the sides of the tub. I was incredibly lucky that I didn't come down on that wineglass.

My heart was racing, but the little girl was just standing there, looking as though she herself had just stepped out of the bath, clothes and all. She couldn't have been even ten years old, and she was wearing shorts and sneakers, and a T-shirt with a unicorn on it, and she had a bicycle helmet on her head, all dripping wet.

"What the hell are you doing here?" I demanded, surprised that my voice worked, thinking *Damn country manners*...

But then I *really* looked at her face.

It was gray, and there was a smear of blood around her nose and mouth despite how wet she was.

Nobody could be that gray, I realized, no matter how badly she was hurt. Nobody *alive* could be that gray.

I had just yelled at a dead girl. A dead girl was standing in my bathroom.

I backed up as far away as I could, into the corner of the tub. If I could have fit down the drain, I would have tried that. Instead I grabbed the shower curtain and tried to wrap myself in that. (Fat lot of protection a vinyl sheet would provide.)

I fought my inclination to just sit there and scream. I could barely get my voice above a squeak. "Who are you?" I asked. "What do you want?"

She stood there a moment longer, water running off her hair, a drop of blood quivering on the end of her chin, then she turned and walked out of the bathroom.

Go, go, go, I mentally urged her.

But once she was gone, I thought, *Where did she go?* and *What's she doing?*

I wanted to stay in the bathroom. I wanted to get out of the tub and lock the bathroom door and wait for my parents to get home.

A locked door might keep Danny out, or even Norman Bates, but what good was a locked door against a ghost?

I got out of the tub carefully.

I grabbed a towel and poked my head out the door. Wet footprints went down the hall and into my room. Should I try running past my room, down the stairs, outside? Should I stand in the street trying to flag down traffic with only a towel wrapped around me and explain to whoever stopped that there was a ghost in my house?

She's just a little girl, I told myself. *She's a ghost, but she's a ghost of a little girl.* That was more sad than scary.

I followed the wet footsteps down the hall and into my room, where they showed up even better on the wood floor. They stopped in front of the closet. And she was not there.

Did I really want to open those doors?

The girl, I told myself, was obviously dead. What harm could she do me? And she had asked for help. I was sure it had been her on the phone the day before. A dead girl was asking me for help.

34

I put my hand on the door handle. Still, I hesitated, bracing myself for ... I didn't know what.

Just do it.

I flung the door open.

My clothes hung exactly as I had set them up the day before.

Or, at least, they *seemed* to.

I took one step in, but then I took a hasty step out. *Yeah, right,* I thought, *go inside, and she might slam the door shut, trapping you in there.*

At the same time I chided myself for being a coward.

As well as overly suspicious—the closet doesn't have a lock.

Still, I got my desk chair and propped one of the doors open. Since she was substantial enough to leave wet footprints, she was probably substantial enough to knock that chair out of the way—if she wanted to. But at least it would delay her for a second or two, and that might give me enough time to get out.

I stepped into the closet.

Chair and door stayed where they were.

Tentatively I reached out, then I pushed the clothes aside to reveal the back wall.

If she was there, I didn't see her; if she wanted me to notice something, I didn't notice it.

I felt the back and the sides and the floor of the closet. No secret panels. Then I silently berated myself because now I had gotten everything I had touched all wet. Had my things been wet before? Had she stepped into or through the closet? I looked at the suds still on my shoulder and couldn't be sure.

I got dressed, cleaned up the bathroom, and put the wineglass back into the kitchen cabinet with the other glasses. I was lucky it had survived being dropped. *Sorry, Mom*, I would have had to explain, *I was sneaking a glass of wine, and it broke when I was startled by a ghost.* Then I would have to assure her, *No, no—I just drank half a glass before I saw her.*

Right.

I stood in the kitchen, looking out the window at the pond. Should I go there? Had that been her I'd seen, trying to get my attention?

No, I thought, not the pond.

If she needed me, she was going to have to come to me in the house—the pond was just too creepy.

The phone rang—the phone that hadn't been connected yet—and at the same time I heard from outside the ringing of that bicycle bell. I yanked open the back door.

There was a girl standing there. But she wasn't the same girl I'd just seen. This one was about my age, and she was standing with her hand raised as though she was about to knock. She took a quick step backward.

"Don't shoot!" she cried, pretending to be even more

startled than she was. She held her hands up, even though in one hand she was balancing a foil-covered plate. "If you don't like zucchini brownies, I promise never to bring them again."

"Sorry," I said. "I just..." I craned to look beyond her, but there was no sign of anybody on a bicycle, and I couldn't hear the bell anymore. For that matter, the phone had stopped ringing, too.

The girl at the door was looking at me with raised eyebrows.

"Sorry," I repeated lamely.

She turned to see what I could have been looking at. Who knows what she thought. "Were you waiting for someone? Did I come at a bad time?"

"No," I said.

Not a friendly opening, but she said, "I'm Michelle Shumway, from next door." She held the plate out to me. "*Do* you like zucchini brownies?"

"I don't know," I admitted doubtfully.

"Well, zucchini brownies are like zucchini in the same sense carrot cake is like carrots," she told me.

"I like carrot cake," I said. It seemed rude to just take the plateful of goodies and close the door on her. "Want to come in?" I offered. "My parents and brother aren't here." That made me sound like a little kid; I added, "So if we decide we really like the brownies, we can eat them all before they get home, and they'll never know what they missed." *Not likely,* I thought, not holding out much hope for a dessert made from vegetables.

The girl—Michelle—grinned. I decided I liked her face. "Oh," she assured me, "there's *always* more zucchini."

"I'm Brenda Keehn," I said as I went to get plates and milk.

"And you just moved in yesterday," she said. There were lots of ways she could have known that, but she added, "My brother Alec was spying on you with his binoculars while you were unloading the truck. Mom caught him at it and took the binoculars away, but he says there's a boy here about his age."

"My brother, Danny, is eleven," I said.

"Alec is twelve. I'm hoping somebody will invent suspended animation soon so that I can freeze him until I'm old enough to move out. Twelve to eighteen is absolutely unbearable in little boys, take my word for it. I have three brothers, and I'd like to donate all their bodies to science."

"Oh yeah," I agreed, "except that Danny became unbearable around ten." Casually I asked, "Was that one of your brothers ringing the bicycle bell before?"

"When?" Michelle asked, but before I could answer, she was already shaking her head. "Well, whenever, no. Alec is the youngest, and I don't think any of them ever had a bell. Patrick has one of those ah-wooo-ga horns on his car, but that's not the same at all."

"No," I agreed.

I was going to let the subject drop, but Michelle added, "And the Wilcoxes on the other side of you are too old for bicycle bells, too."

"Oh, well," I said. It wasn't trying to change the subject that made me say, "These brownies are good." They *were*, I was surprised to find—moist and chocolatey.

Michelle smiled and nodded, by which I guessed she had made them, not her mother. I can make brownies, too, but only from a box mix. Michelle went back to telling me what her brother had discovered about us: "So there's you and Danny, and both your parents?" Just the slightest emphasis on *both*, as though that was what she was checking.

"Yeah. They teach."

"At the high school?"

"Community college."

"They start in a couple weeks," she said. "We get a week and a half more. I'm starting junior year; how about you?"

I nodded.

"Great," she said. And it would be nice to have at least one familiar face to look for. Whether or not we were in a one-room schoolhouse.

"Tell me about you," I said.

"Well, I'm the second to the youngest of five, unfortunately all of them boys except for me and Rachel, who really doesn't count because she's so damn old she's forgotten what it's like to be a kid. My mother is a visiting nurse, my father skipped out on the family years ago, and I've lived in the same house all my life."

She was discreetly looking around the kitchen.

"I love what you've done with this place already," she said. "It was getting to be a real wreck before, but you've fixed it up nice." She stood and followed the hose from the sink to the doorway. "A lot of plants upstairs that need watering?"

I laughed. "Water bed," I explained.

"Yeah? Me, too," she said, which surprised me—I would have figured a straw-stuffed mattress with a goose-down comforter, handmade by her grandmother from the down of her family's own geese. She asked, "So where did you move from?"

"Buffalo."

"Must be neat living in a big city like Buffalo," Michelle said wistfully, as though we were talking about New York or Paris. "Sometimes it's so annoying living in a small town. Everybody knows everybody, and everybody knows everybody's family. Like it's not bad enough having my teachers say, 'When your sister, Rachel, was in this class...' some of them remember when they taught my *mother*. And everybody has you pegged by your family, so they'll say, 'Oh, those Shumways, they never amount to anything,' or 'Those Lyons girls never can pick a man that'll stay around for longer than it takes to father a litter of kids.' My mother's a Lyons. At least we're not Doolittles, who have to hear people say, 'The Doolittles do little,' a million times a year, with everybody thinking they're being *so* original. You're lucky—your family will be newcomers for at least a couple generations before people admit you're going to stay in Westport and come up with some way to describe you besides 'the new uns.'"

I didn't tell her that I only planned on being in Westport for two years. Actually, I thought she was kind of funny and fun. I liked the way she seemed willing to say anything.

I helped myself to a second brownie.

Michelle had been waiting for me before she accepted a second helping herself.

"So you knew the people who lived here before?" I asked.

"Yup," Michelle said.

"Any little kids?" I didn't ask, *Any little kids who died?* but I was sure she was going to tell me all about it.

"Nope," Michelle said. "Old Mrs. Reinhardt was renting it out to a bunch of students from the college for the last twenty years or so." She flashed her quick grin. "Not the same students for the whole twenty years," she clarified.

"And before that?" I asked, but already I was thinking, *Kids didn't wear bicycle helmets like that twenty years ago, did they?*

"Before that," Michelle said, "old *Mr.* Reinhardt was alive."

"They have any kids?"

"About a zillion years ago."

So who was that little girl I had seen? And why was she haunting *this* house?

Having finished her second brownie, Michelle said, "A bunch of us were going to go to the community pool. Want to come?"

"There's a community pool?" I asked.

"Sure. We don't spend *every* afternoon riding around in the back of our pickups shooting woodchucks."

I laughed, though that was pretty close to the picture I had of how teenagers in the sticks would pass the time.

The ghost had contacted me once by phone, once by the pond, once in my water bed, and once in the bathtub. Three out of four times near water. Much as I thought Michelle and I might well eventually become friends, it was too early for me to tell her why I didn't dare go to a public pool—not till I found out what was going on, and why.

"I'd really, really, really like to go," I told her. "I am *not* brushing you off—please, please, please ask me again some other time."

"Humph!" she snorted, tossing her head as though insulted. But then she grinned and said, "Sure. Send your little brother over to meet my little brother. If they have each other to play with, maybe they'll spend less time tormenting us."

After she left I went upstairs to check on the progress of my water bed, and that was when I remembered that I was wrong: I hadn't had *four* encounters with the ghost—I'd had five. For there were my clothes, once more lying on the floor. This time there were muddy footprints where she had stomped on them.

The ghost said she wanted help, but she also seemed to have a temper.

Despite the effort my father had put into preparing the water bed for me—twice now—I slept in the extra bed in the computer room. Dad rolled his eyes and said, "Fine"; Danny asked if *he* could have the water bed, and I was tempted to inflict it on him; and Mom said, "Good night."

I woke up to the sound of a bell ringing—a bicycle bell. I opened my eyes and saw that there was an odd light in the room. Not the light of dawn coming through the window, or the light from the hallway coming underneath the door. I could make out the numbers on my wristwatch, which I'd put on the nightstand before climbing into bed: 1:23. That would be A.M.

I turned my head slowly.

The light was coming from the computer monitor screens. Both of them were on. Do I need to mention I hadn't turned them on before going to bed? What was this ghost's thing about one o'clock in the morning?

I got up and looked. The little girl's face stared back at me from both screens. She was still dripping water. But she *had* changed. I quickly averted my eyes. She was more obviously dead than before: Bits of her skin were missing; she was decomposing.

"What do you want?" I asked.

When she didn't answer, I stole a quick glance at her. She was just looking at me, swaying slightly as little kids do—the kind who can't hold still for a moment. *Not fair,* I told myself as I caught myself in that thought. *She IS still, wherever her body is. She's still and she will be from now on, until her body*... Well, that wasn't a good thought, because her body evidently already *was* starting to...

"If you aren't going to be more helpful at this hour of the night...," I whispered to her.

I would have turned off the computers, but they weren't turned on. So I tossed my blanket over the monitors, the way people do to get their pet birds to sleep.

Eventually the bicycle-bell ringing stopped.

The good country-air smell did not.

The next morning I was vaguely aware of my parents getting up and going out. I knew they had meetings with the department heads at the college to talk about their upcoming classes, but that was no reason *I* had to get up.

I heard the car doors slam, then the crunch of gravel as their car pulled out of the driveway. I'm not sure if a little or a lot of time passed, but then somebody was knocking on the computer room door.

"Go away," I mumbled.

"Brenda?" It was Danny. "Brenda, I'm going over to meet that guy Alec."

"Good," I called, if it would get him out of the house. Since when did he check in with me?

Danny said, "But I wanted you to know I didn't have anything to do with it."

I gathered enough energy to ask, "*What* are you talking about?"

"I thought you were up already," he said, "because I heard you in your room—your own room. But when I passed by here, I saw that you were still in here. And then when I went by your room to go downstairs, the door was partway open and I peeked in, so I came back to tell you: I didn't have anything to do with it."

I didn't like the sound of that.

As soon as Danny heard my feet hit the floor, he took off running down the stairs, obviously wanting to be out of the house before I investigated.

What now?

Actually it was the same old thing, but more so. My clothes were once again out of the closet, but this time some of the plastic hangers were broken and the wire ones twisted, two of my blouses were ripped, and she had evidently wiped her wet and bloody face against my favorite dress. "What do you want?" I screamed at her.

The phone rang.

I ran downstairs, picked it up, and shouted, "Leave me alone!" then slammed the phone back down.

It rang again.

Be calm, I told myself. *She's a little girl, and she's dead, and she's frightened and confused.* Never mind that she was frightening and confusing me. I picked up the phone, but I couldn't summon up anything more sympathetic than a snarled "What?"

There was a slight pause, but at least she didn't ring her stupid bicycle bell at me.

Then a man's voice spoke: "Telephone company. I've checked the wires to the pole. Just calling to say you're all hooked up."

I glanced out the kitchen window and could see him perched on his pole, his company truck at the edge of our driveway.

"Thank you," I managed to say. How could I apologize without making myself out to be even more of a loser: *I thought you were someone else*—when he'd just connected the line?

I went back upstairs to pick up my room, yet again, and got dressed. I jammed the ruined clothes into the back of the closet, behind a box of winter clothes. I'd deal with them later.

As I was making up the bed I had used in the spare room, I could hear a humming and realized the computers were on.

I took off the blanket I'd thrown on last night and saw, once again, the little girl who had been appearing to me. But this time she looked a lot better. This time she looked not only dry but alive — and smiling.

Then I realized it wasn't her — it was a *picture* of her. I clicked on the button to reduce the size of the picture and saw I was looking at the site of the electronic edition of the *Buffalo Herald*. The picture was part of an article: NEIGHBORS RALLY IN SEARCH FOR LEAH-ANN.

I read the article. An eight-year-old girl named Leah-Ann Maitland had been missing since some time between six-thirty and eleven-thirty Friday night. Leah-Ann's mother was quoted as saying that she had sent Leah-Ann to her room after the two of them had argued at dinner because Leah-Ann wanted to spend the night at a friend's house. But when Mrs. Maitland herself was ready to go to bed after the eleven o'clock news, she discovered that Leah-Ann was missing. She called the friend's house, but Leah-Ann had not shown up there. Mrs. Maitland walked the two blocks to the friend's house, but there was no sign of Leah-Ann along the way. Next she called her ex-husband, Leah-Ann's father, who lived about five miles away. No Leah-Ann there, either. Then they called the police.

I hadn't heard about any of this, because Friday night had been my last night in Buffalo. By the time it was on the Saturday news, we had already packed the last of our stuff into two cars and a van and were taking off for the manure-tilled fields of eastern upstate New York.

Apparently at first the police hoped that Leah-Ann had run away and had gotten lost on her way to her father's—after all, she was only eight and had never before been there on her own. But that hope waned as she didn't show up Saturday, and she didn't show up Sunday. "We're still hopeful," a police spokesperson was quoted as saying. "The fact that her bicycle is missing is a good sign because it may well indicate that she was not abducted from her home but has run away." But the unspoken question was clear: If she simply had gotten lost, or even if she had been hurt—where was she? And why hadn't her bicycle turned up?

Her bicycle, I thought. That explained the bell, and the helmet.

The article ended with another quote from the police: "At least the weather is on our side. She's not in danger of exposure."

I sat down heavily on the edge of the bed.

Oh crap. Exposure was the least of her worries. She was dead, and I was the only one who knew it.

Or...

Or maybe I wasn't. *Had* she been abducted? I wondered. Had she set off for her father's, and some creep picked her up? Picked her up, killed her, and dropped her body off somewhere near here? I thought of her face, gray and bloody. *Poor little thing.*

But what could *I* do? Call the hot-line number and say that maybe they might want to search in Westport because the missing girl's dead spirit was hanging around nearly a hundred fifty miles from the search area?

I glanced out the window. The computer room is on the end of the house, so that one window looks over the side yard and one over the back. Out of the back window, I could see the pond.

...And the ghost—Leah-Ann—standing there, looking up at me.

"Wait there!" I yelled. Shouting orders to a ghost. Intentionally going out of my way to meet a ghost. But how else was I going to find out what she wanted and get her—eventually—to stop coming to me?

I ran downstairs, out the back door, into the yard.

Amazingly, she was still there, though she was beginning to move, heading off toward the driveway, toward the neighbors I now knew to be the Shumways. I took off after her, but she didn't go to the Shumways'; she drifted into our garage. I was sure she would pull her disappearing act again, the way she had with my closet, so I called, "How can I help you if you keep going away?"

Sure enough, when I stepped into the garage, I couldn't see her. But in a moment my eyes adjusted to the shadows, after the bright sunlight, and there she was, standing with her back to the Honda, as though I'd trapped her. The water still dripped off the ends of her hair that hung below her bicycle helmet. Her face was... worse than before.

I tried not to appear disgusted—how could that not distress her?—but it was so hard to look at her. "What do you want from me?" I asked.

She put her hand to her throat. Did she need the technology of the unconnected phone to make her voice heard? Or—since her ghost body obviously reflected the state of her real body—was she unable to speak anymore because the soft tissues inside her throat had disintegrated already?

In the silence a fear started in the pit of my stomach: that the reason she didn't answer was because she knew I wouldn't like what she had to say.

What was the worst possible thing she could want? What was the last thing in the world I would want to face doing? I shuddered. "You want me to tell your parents, don't you? So they don't keep wondering..." Was *won-*

dering the right word? "Hoping..." That didn't seem quite it either. "Dreading..."

Apparently my dithering ticked her off. The ghost that had been Leah-Ann whirled around. Viciously she kicked the Honda's fender. And in the same moment, she disappeared—not in a puff of vapor or a quick dissolve, just... gone.

"Jeez," I muttered. I leaned in and even in the dim light saw that there was a dent right where the fender met the bumper. "Nasty little thing, aren't you?" I was tempted to call out that if she was going to be like that— ripping my clothes, damaging my parents' car—then she could find somebody else to help her. But I couldn't bring myself to say it. If I were dead and scared, I'd want somebody to be patient with me... even if being dead had made me surly—which I had to believe it would.

"Always talk to yourself?" a voice behind me asked.

I whirled around and saw Michelle peeking into the garage.

Which might be why Leah-Ann got peeved and took off, I thought, once my brain reconnected and I could breathe again.

Not wanting Michelle to see how startled I'd been, not wanting to explain, I answered, "Only if there's nobody else to talk to." And before she could ask any more questions, I suggested, "Come to the house and have some zucchini brownies? A nice neighbor girl brought some over yesterday, between plowing the fields and cooking up squirrel meat."

"Those country gals sure know how to have fun," Michelle said.

Sitting around the kitchen seemed too much like the farm family in *Lassie*, so I invited her into the living room, but that was a mistake. The bad smell of the past two days was even worse there.

"Oh," I said, taking a hasty step back and waving my hand in front of my nose. "Do they ever stop fertilizing?"

Michelle brushed past me into the living room. "That's not fertilizing," she said, sniffing. "That smells like something died."

My stomach felt like it dropped to my knees.

Leah-Ann. That was why she was hanging around here. She *had* been abducted. And her killer had dumped her body...

I thought I was going to throw up. It was bad enough seeing a decomposing ghost. The thought that her actual body was here, all this while, near enough to smell...

Michelle had swept out of the living room, out of the house.

I didn't blame her.

But she wasn't going home. I saw her cross the yard, staring at the ground near the house, poking at the bushes.

She's looking to see what's causing the smell, I realized.

She thought it was an animal, and she was going to find the body of a poor little dead girl.

Even country folk couldn't be used to that.

"Michelle, wait!" I cried. I set down the tray with our brownies and milk and ran outside.

My parents were just pulling up in the car. Frantically I waved them over.

Michelle was crouched down by the overgrown hydrangeas, which didn't look to have been cut back in years.

"Don't!" I called to her.

"Raccoon," she said.

"What?"

"Like they don't smell bad enough when they're alive."

I said, "A raccoon died in our bushes?" I was so sure she was wrong—and was seeing maybe just the back of Leah-Ann's head—that I didn't dare look.

"Could be a fox." Michelle cocked her head for a better look. "But probably not."

By then my father had crossed the lawn. "What's up?"

"Dead raccoon," Michelle told him.

My father looked and made a face. But it was definitely a seeing-a-dead-animal-that-had-to-be-dealt-with face, not a seeing-a-dead-girl face. "I'll get a shovel," he said.

"I'm going to be sick," I said.

But at least I made it to the bathroom first.

———

That afternoon Dad went to this place called Zicardi Brothers to get the Honda tuned up and aligned. I wondered if he would notice the dent in the fender. I could just picture myself explaining, "An angry ghost girl kicked it." Yeah, right. Since that was the car I used, my parents would be sure to figure *I* was to blame. But if he didn't notice until *after* today, maybe he would think one of the Zicardi brothers had done it.

Mom knocked on my bedroom door and stuck her head in. Michelle and I were trying on different makeups and were playing CDs so loud, it was probably the second or third time Mom had knocked. "What's this?" she asked.

When I saw what she was holding, I had trouble keeping my face from showing panic. I pretended I couldn't see what was in her hand. "What have you got?" I asked, stalling for time by lowering the volume of the music. Oh-so-lightly I added, "And where did you get it?"

To answer the first part, Mom stepped closer to show me. To the second part, she answered, "I found it on my dresser. Did you put it there?"

On her dresser?

Did *I* put it on her dresser?

"It" was a student ID card for one Isobel Gehris of the State University of New York at Fredonia, whose birthday was early enough in the year that she was legally allowed to buy alcohol.

"I..." I shook my head.

Mom shrugged. "Danny must have found it," she said, "in the back of his closet or under the grate of the cold-air return." She pondered it a bit more. "One of the students who lived here must have lost it." She caught herself, for that wouldn't make sense. Fredonia is one hour farther away than Buffalo—quite a daily commute. Still trying to make sense of it, she speculated, "Or someone from Fredonia was visiting one of the kids here." She kept on looking at the card, trying to figure it out.

Don't be helpful, I wanted to beg her. *Don't call Fredonia to try to track this girl down to return it.*

"Oh, well," Mom said.

If I was lucky, she would forget to ask Danny.

At least she hadn't found it in my jeans pocket, which was the last place *I* had put it, because Isobel Gehris looks very much like I do when I wear the right makeup and if I part my hair in the middle.

Behind me the closet door rattled.

But only once.

"Whoa," Michelle said. "Spooks."

A spook, indeed, who tore through my clothes and put what she found on Mom's dresser.

There was a knock at the room's door, and all three of us jumped. But it was only Dad. He didn't seem surprised to find Mom there, and he didn't seem to notice the ID card in her hand. "Brenda," he said to me.

He'd found the dent where Leah-Ann had kicked the car, I could tell, and he thought that I had done it.

"Michelle," he said, "my wife and I need to talk to Brenda."

Michelle, who could smell trouble as surely as she could smell dead raccoons, got out of there fast.

Dad reached over and turned off the CD player. He said, "Brenda—"

"I know you're going to find this hard to believe," I interrupted. *I* found it hard to believe, and didn't know how to start.

"What?" Mom prompted.

Dad said, "The people at the shop say the Honda has been in an accident."

Oh, great, I thought. *It wasn't even him that noticed.*

Mom was looking from Dad to me. "What kind of accident?"

How could I ever get them to believe it was a ghost-kicking-the-fender accident?

Slowly, Dad said, "They had the car up on the lift... And they showed me underneath..."

Underneath?

Dad took a breath and started over again. "They say it looks like something was run over..."

Mom echoed, "'Something'? Like a bottle?" She had her concentrating expression on. "Or..."

"Bigger," Dad said. "They had someone from the collision department look at it. He's seen a lot of accidents, and he said right away that something big was hit. Then he found a piece of plastic caught around the shaft, like one of those tassel streamers kids sometimes have on their bicycle handlebars."

I could hardly breathe. "Not a bicycle," I said. All I had hit had been the curb on the edge of the pavement.

"There was some blood," Dad finished. "They think someone might have gotten hurt."

I shook my head. "I didn't..." I couldn't get my voice to work. "I didn't run over anyone on a bicycle," I protested. I *hadn't*. I knew that.

"Where did you go Friday night?" Dad asked.

"To Traci's," I said.

"Directly to Traci's?" he asked. "And did you stay there the whole evening?"

I hadn't had an accident with the car. I *knew* I hadn't.

"We went to pick up Jennie," I admitted—which I wasn't supposed to have done. They had only given me permission to go to Traci's. "And Tina," I grudgingly added. Tina lived way over in Amherst. I wasn't even supposed to be driving after dark, but they had said I could go say good-bye to Traci, four streets over, if I drove carefully. I always drive carefully.

"Did you stay at Tina's?" Dad asked.

"No," I admitted. "We went to the park." This was all so confusing. What had Leah-Ann done to me?

For the first time Dad glanced at the ID in Mom's hand. Apparently he saw the resemblance right away. Very quietly he asked, "Were you drinking?"

"A little bit," I said, figuring I was in enough trouble, I'd better be honest. "But I didn't have an accident."

Dad looked gray. Not as gray as Leah-Ann but definitely not well. Mom was crying, soundlessly, the tears pouring down her cheeks, as Dad said, "The people at the car shop are going to be reporting this to the police in Buffalo. The police in Buffalo will have to take a look at all the hit-and-run accidents—"

"I didn't hit anyone!" I cried. The police in Buffalo had enough to worry about with trying to find Leah-Ann. "We only bought a couple six-packs. Well, three. But I drove very, very carefully."

I *had*. We were just driving around, listening to tapes and feeling sorry because it was the last time we were all going to be together.

I remember fighting, playfully, with Tina, who wasn't as crazy about hearing "Margaritaville" over and over again as I was. I kept rewinding the tape because it seemed the perfect song for a summer night of good-byes, and after a while she got sick of it and she hit FAST FORWARD, and then I hit REWIND, and she hit the button to play the other side, and while I was trying to find "Margaritaville" again I accidentally turned the volume up so loud it hurt our ears, so Jennie and Traci both scrambled up from the backseat to lean over to adjust the volume, and we swerved off the road—we were on Hopkins, where it follows Ransom Creek, and there aren't any lights and there isn't any shoulder—so it was like hitting a speed bump when the car went off the road, just for an instant, then another bump and we were back on again, so that Traci and Jennie put their hands up like you do when you're riding a roller coaster, and Tina smacked her head against the dashboard, because she was leaning forward to mess with the buttons some more, and she said if she had any short-term memory loss she was going to have to sue me, but she didn't get hurt, and we didn't hit anything. Or run over anything. Not that I knew of.

Wouldn't you know if you had done something like run over someone?

Wouldn't you know if you had killed somebody?

I still don't remember seeing her. I don't remember being aware of hitting her. I would have stopped if I had known.

I didn't look in the rearview mirror and see her try to get back up on the bike the way the police say she must have done. I didn't see her wobble and fall into the bushes and into the creek beyond.

The only reason I knew to tell you to look in the creek where it comes right up to Hopkins at that last curve is because when I saw Leah-Ann—when she came to me after she was dead—she was always wet. She was dead and she was wet and she kept coming to me because I was the only one who could help her.

I didn't know.

END OF RECORDING

Brenda Keehn

transcript signed by Brenda Keehn

Eugene Randolph

in the presence of Eugene Randolph, Attorney-at-Law

Dancing with
Marjorie's Ghost

Nobody was surprised when Conrad Sharpe's wife, Marjorie, died.

Conrad Sharpe was a mean man—a bully and a bragger. He was too lazy and too stingy to fix the roof that leaked in the spring or the door and window frames that let in the howling winter wind, but he expected his wife to keep the house warm and comfortable. Her hands were rough and red from working in the house and working in the yard. All day long she worked, and late into the night. The neighbors always said that for each year Marjorie spent married to Conrad, she seemed to age two.

So no one was surprised when—one cold gray day as autumn turned to winter—Marjorie Sharpe died. The neighbors said it was the only way Marjorie could get any rest.

But, oh, how Conrad wept at Marjorie's funeral.

Conrad Sharpe always liked to be the best at everything — the biggest, the loudest, the fastest: the best. And if he'd never thought to be the best husband, why, that was no reason he couldn't be the best widower.

He went to Kelly's General Store and bought the most expensive suit for everyone to see him in and the most expensive dress to lay Marjorie out in. He bought the most expensive coffin from Gilbert Allen's casket shop, and he threw himself on the casket when the undertaker closed the lid, because Conrad Sharpe wanted to make sure everybody saw what a fine casket it was. He was careful, though, not to wrinkle his new suit.

Conrad wailed and sobbed and carried on all the while the casket was lowered into the ground, so that everyone would know what a devoted husband he had been.

Then he invited everyone back to the house afterward, for food and drink and to remember Marjorie, though he'd never been willing to pay for a party while Marjorie had been alive.

"Oh, Marjorie, poor Marjorie," Conrad said to the neighbors. "Do you remember how she loved to dance?"

The neighbors remembered. They remembered Marjorie dancing *before* she married Conrad.

"There never seemed to be enough time for dancing," Conrad said, though the truth was he was too disagreeable to like music and dancing. "Oh, if only Marjorie could come back for even one night," Conrad cried out, "I swear I'd dance with her to her heart's content."

A cold wind came howling then, where none had been before. Noisily it shook the boards of the Sharpes' house, and came in through the cracks by the windows, and down the chimney, and blew out the candle by Conrad's chair.

And then went away.

In the sudden stillness, Conrad realized everyone was looking at him. He rubbed at his eyes and repeated, "If only Marjorie could come back for even one night, I swear I'd dance with her to her heart's content."

Way, way down the street, the neighbors' dogs started barking.

Then, closer neighbors' dogs started barking.

And closer.

And closer.

Till the next-door neighbor's dog was barking.

Till there was a sound, like someone scratching at the Sharpes' front door.

The neighbors all looked at one another, and at Conrad.

To prove his courage, Conrad got out of his chair by the blown-out candle and walked to the door and opened it.

There was nothing there....

Except on the dusting of snow that had covered the

front walk since everyone had come in, there were foot-prints, footprints that came from down the street, up the front walk, and ended at the door.

With no one there.

His hands shaking, Conrad closed the door. And bolted it. And said, a third time—to prove that he was cold, not afraid—"If only Marjorie could come back for even one night, I swear I'd dance with her to her heart's content."

The door flew open, bursting lock and wood alike.

There stood Marjorie Sharpe in her fine new dress, though she had no shoes—since they wouldn't show in the casket, penny-pinching Conrad had buried her with bare feet. Her hair was unbound and streamed out behind her, and though she was pale, she looked more beautiful than she had in years.

With never a word, she held her arms out to her hus-band.

And Conrad—to prove he was the bravest man there—asked, "Why, woman, would you come back from the grave to dance with me?"

Silently, solemnly, Marjorie nodded, and Conrad stepped forward. He put his arms about her body, which was as cold and as hard as the autumn-turning-to-winter ground, and together—while the neighbors watched with eyes gone wide in terror—Marjorie and Conrad Sharpe danced.

Around and around they went on Marjorie's well-swept floor, to music none of the neighbors could hear. Or maybe they danced to the howling of the neighbors' dogs.

After an hour Conrad said, "You came back for one night, and we danced. Surely we've danced to your heart's content," and he made to step away.

But Marjorie wouldn't let go, and Marjorie wouldn't stop dancing.

One hour turned to two, and the dogs continued to howl and the Sharpes continued to dance, while the neighbors watched with bodies made heavy with terror, till the candles burned low and the clock struck midnight. Then Conrad said, "You came back for one night, and we danced all night. Surely we've danced to your heart's content," and he made to push Marjorie away.

But still Marjorie wouldn't let go, and Marjorie wouldn't stop dancing.

Hour after hour the dogs continued to howl and the Sharpes continued to dance, while the neighbors watched with minds made numb by terror, till the candles burned out, past the setting of the moon, till the sky began to grow light with dawn. Then, pleased with himself, for he was sure that he had gotten the best of Marjorie's ghost, Conrad said, "You came back for one night, and we danced all night and into the next day. Surely you've danced to your heart's content," and this time he gave Marjorie a great shove.

But still Marjorie wouldn't let go, and still Marjorie wouldn't stop dancing. She danced Conrad out the door, no matter how he struggled, and down the front walk and into the street.

None of the neighbors dared follow, and the last they saw of Conrad was through the open door; they saw his pale face, and they saw the tails of his new coat blowing in the wind as he danced with Marjorie down the street.

A few minutes later, all at once, the neighbors' dogs stopped barking.

Once the sun was high in the sky, the neighbors followed the footprints in the snow. Down the street those footprints led, and over the hill, and they didn't stop till they came to the cemetery, where the dirt was mounded neatly over Marjorie Sharpe's new grave, just as it had been left the day before.

And there the footprints stopped.

In the years that followed, come cold dark nights as autumn turned to winter, the townspeople often asked themselves what had become of Conrad. But no one dared dig up Marjorie's grave to learn the truth, for fear of what they might see.

Shadow Brother

My brother, Kevin, may or may not have come back from the dead for any one of several contradictory reasons, depending on which of my relatives you assume is most reasonable. Personally, I wouldn't consider any of us particularly reliable.

Since Kevin was a boy, and since he was born five years before I was, we had few common interests. That meant we didn't consider each other competition, and that, for the most part, kept us from finding it useful or especially gratifying to persecute each other.

The only time he was put in charge of me was when I was in first grade and my parents told him he had to walk me to and from school. This he did without trying to lose me. No running and cutting through people's backyards and climbing fences, which some of my friends' brothers (and sisters) did.

I submit that as Exhibit A in the case against Kevin becoming a malevolent ghost. (Though I'd be the first to admit that death changes everything.)

When I was in second grade, the people three houses down got a dog that would come to the very edge of their yard and growl whenever I passed. Though Kevin was no longer officially in charge of me, he put himself between me and that dog, and he growled back. The dog slunk away. From then on that dog knew I knew he was a coward, and he didn't bother me anymore, even when Kevin wasn't with me.

Exhibit B. For anyone who's keeping track.

For all of that, Kevin and I didn't think alike: I was a fan of the Beatles; he liked the Rolling Stones. My favorite TV show was *Dr. Kildare*; Kevin said Ben Casey was the better doctor and *The Defenders* was a better show. But different tastes in music and TV are not important. One of the big ways we differed was our reactions when our father talked about being in France during World War II. Dad had been part of the OSS. His group would parachute behind enemy lines to help the French Resistance fighters, and one of his stories was about the time one of his men landed badly, breaking a leg. They couldn't bring the wounded man with them, because he would have slowed them down. And they couldn't leave him behind, because if he was captured the Germans would surely torture him until he revealed the men's hiding place. So Dad had to shoot him. His own man.

I hoped I would never find myself in a position where I had to kill one of my friends, but I also hoped that—if I had to—I could be as strong as my father.

But when I made the mistake of sharing this profound thought with Kevin, he called me a ninny. The women, he pointed out, stayed home and kept the factories going, except for the Wacs and Waves, who were mostly nurses, and nobody expected them to shoot anybody.

"In France," I pointed out, "the women fought."

"Oh, good heavens!" Kevin gasped, an expression he normally did *not* use. "I *thought* you might be turning French, Sarah, but I wasn't sure. We'll have to keep you away from French bread and frogs' legs until you get over it."

Kevin never seemed to be interested in hearing what he called "the old war stories"—our parents' or our aunts' and uncles'. Not even Aunt Lise's, who was born in Germany and had different stories from everybody else's. Like how by the end of the war she and her mother were eating grass from what had been their front yard, because all the supplies went to support the German military, not the civilians. She claimed Uncle Jack had saved her life by marrying her and bringing her to America after his tour of duty was up. And that was despite the fact that, when she first got here, Americans who recognized her accent sometimes spat at her, even though she was barely eighteen and too young to have had anything to do with the war.

I thought all this stuff was fascinating. While I would stay indoors after dinners with the aunts and uncles, lapping it all up, Kevin would go play basketball with his friends.

Would a disinterest in the past be a sign that Kevin was not likely to ever turn into a ghost? Exhibit C? Or at least Exhibit B and a half?

One time, when I was ten and Kevin was fifteen, Dad wouldn't let Kevin escape. Kevin made some comment criticizing the growing U.S. involvement in Vietnam, and that made Dad mad. "Fascists, Nazis, Communists; they're all the same," Dad said, and the next Sunday he asked Uncle Jack to "Bring those pictures." "Those pictures" were ones Uncle Jack had taken when he had been with a group that had liberated one of the concentration camps where the Nazis used to keep Jews. Dad felt Kevin should see them.

Kevin, but not me. And not Uncle Jack and Aunt Lise's son, Dwight, who was one year younger than me. (Dwight was *exactly* the kind of boy who if he died would come back and haunt his family. He would be the sort of ghost who would rattle chains in the attic and who would sneak up behind you and breathe on your neck.)

"Go out and play," Dad told us.

Aunt Lise agreed with him. "These pictures are disturbing. They are not for you to see."

Well, all right. Be that way.

Dwight and I could wait.

We went up to Kevin's room and played Monopoly, but we listened until we heard Uncle Jack open the hall closet door to return the pictures to his coat pocket. Then I sent Dwight downstairs to fetch a glass of milk, and on his way back he stopped at the closet.

The pictures were worse than disturbing. I felt scummy, as though I was looking at dirty pictures, as though—by looking at those pictures—I was responsible for what was in them. I'd never seen such skinny people, not even in the pictures of starving African kids that the nuns would show us on Mission Sunday.

"They don't even look real," I said.

"Maybe they're actors," Dwight suggested. With Dwight it was sometimes hard to tell if he was joking or being stupid.

The men all had shaven heads; the women all had scarves to hide that their heads had been shaved, too. And there were kids, as bald and dull-eyed as the grown-ups. I'd seen pictures of other people—French and Belgian and Egyptian—welcoming the liberating troops. They were always waving, cheering, dancing in the streets. There was always some young woman climbing up on the tanks to kiss the soldiers. The people from *this* camp just stood there, though you'd figure they'd have been the most relieved to be rescued. But they just looked at the camera, or beyond it, with their hollow eyes, as though they'd given up hoping and weren't ready to believe they'd really been rescued.

I couldn't stop looking, even though I wanted to.

Kevin came in then, and he plucked the pictures out of our hands. "These are the ones who were rescued," he reassured me, even though I hadn't said a word. "These guys survived."

I hoped Kevin was right, and ignored the fact that his foot came down on Dwight's before Dwight could talk about the ones who weren't rescued.

Exhibit Whatever.

That was my vision of the war my parents had lived through: the valiant Americans who came in the nick of time to rescue the downtrodden people of the world. Bad was bad and good was good. Once in a while there were hard choices—wounded buddies, no-win situations—but generally if you thought about it long enough, you would know what you had to do if you were brave enough to do it.

Then came the war in Vietnam.

At fourteen I was more interested in trying to iron my hair straight and in reading J. R. R. Tolkien's "Ring" trilogy than in watching the news—especially news that was always depressing. And it wasn't just that American soldiers were getting killed. Buddhist monks were setting themselves on fire to protest the war; college students were burning flags and draft cards and ROTC buildings, yelling and screaming into the TV cameras. I was vaguely annoyed at the rude and messy ruckus, but mostly I was grateful—grateful to be a girl so I wasn't draftable, a Catholic so I could look down my nose at the suicidal Buddhists, and too young to go to college, which looked to be fast becoming a dangerous place to be.

Kevin, of course, *was* draftable.

He was also more sympathetic to the draft dodgers and the protesters—Buddhist and U.S.—than anybody else in the family. Is that another piece of evidence to support that he couldn't have turned into a vengeance-seeking ghost, that he was sympathetic by nature and didn't approve of killing?

Or is it a sign pointing at exactly the opposite?

"When I was your age," Dad told him at the dinner table, the day he got his draft card with a number so low we knew he would be drafted, "I was proud to serve my country."

"When you were my age," Kevin countered, "the United States had been attacked at Pearl Harbor, and Hitler was an obvious psychotic who wanted to take over the world and re-create it in his own image."

"Yeah?" Dad wouldn't have been surprised that his patriotic pep talk was being sidetracked. This was not a new conversation.

"Now, *we're* the bad guys."

I thought, *Can't we talk about something else for a change?* Being stuck at the dinner table, with the conversation endlessly going round and round, the only thing I could think of was *Hey, how about those guys on Ed Sullivan last night who spun all those plates on those poles.* Probably not the most brilliant opening for diverting an argument.

"The bad guys," Dad said, "are the ones who keep undermining their own country—kids who have too much time on their hands and don't appreciate that their parents are going broke sending them to college."

"Have you looked at a map lately?" Kevin asked. "North Vietnam is...what—the size of Florida? Talk about the bully that can't pick on someone his own size."

Mom, spooning out mashed potatoes, murmured, "Kevin, you don't need to be sarcastic to make your point. And, Tom, we're all right here—you don't need to shout to be heard."

"He isn't making a point at all," Dad said, "and I am not shouting." But he did lower his voice. "*Obviously* this isn't an issue between the United States and North Vietnam. Because *if* it were just North Vietnam"—Mom handed me the bowl of potatoes, since Dad was too engrossed in making his own point to take it—"the war would have been over about two and a half minutes after it started. This is an issue of fighting Communism, of keeping the people of the world free."

"What's right for us isn't necessarily right for the world," Kevin said. "Especially when the only leaders they have to choose from are corrupt."

"You don't know what you're talking about," Dad snapped.

Mom cut in. Very sweetly she said, "Well, *none* of us has actually been to Vietnam to see and judge for ourselves."

Dad gave her a look of surprised betrayal.

Mom? *Mom* coming in with what sounded suspiciously like an opinion? I knew where everybody else stood on the Vietnam issue: Dad for military intervention, Kevin against, me for not talking about it anymore. But I realized for the first time that maybe Mom wasn't with me. Maybe, even though she never said anything, she had views of her own. Or maybe not. Maybe she was just trying to make peace in the family.

Still, the heat of the discussion went down several notches. To Kevin, Dad said, "Do you think I wasn't afraid to fight in a war, too?"

"That isn't...," Kevin started in a huff. But then he sighed. "That isn't all of it."

"I know," Dad said. He patted Kevin's hand, awkwardly, self-consciously. "I also know you'll do the right thing."

The old I-know-you'll-do-the-right-thing ploy.

And Dad was right. Despite his dinnertime complaints, Kevin didn't try for conscientious-objector status, nor did he burn his card or take off for Canada, which a couple of the boys in his class did. He reported for service, which Dad took as a victory for his persuasive ability, so Dad forgave Kevin his lack of enthusiasm.

What he couldn't forgive was that Kevin got killed.

The telegram came on a bright summer Saturday. My mother was in the side yard, hanging clothes out to dry. My father was trying to teach tricks to the brain-damaged puppy he had rescued from the animal shelter three weeks earlier and had named—for some reason clear only to my father—Spartacus. I was just sitting around being hot, wondering out loud why if the Fitzhughs next door could afford an air conditioner, we couldn't; and why if Mary Beth Hinkle's family took their vacation in a cottage at Myrtle Beach every year, we only ever went camping at Stony Brook Park.

Then this car pulled up in front of our house. Out came these two army guys in spiffy new uniforms. I think that was when all three of us knew—then, as soon as we saw them, before the army guys said a word, before they started their slow, deliberate walk up the driveway.

Mom came around front, still holding a clothespin in one hand and a pillowcase in the other. Dad pushed

Spartacus away, and when Spartacus kept on trying to pull the stick from Dad's hand, Dad broke it in two and let the pieces drop. I stood up from the stoop, thinking, *This is so like Mary Beth, to be off at the beach when I need her here.*

Kevin—the army men and the telegram explained— had been killed when his unit had been ambushed by the Vietcong. There weren't very many more details available, other than that five other men had been killed at the same time.

"*Men*"? I thought, surprised to hear the term applied to Kevin. Kevin wasn't a man: He was my brother. *Fathers* are men. *Uncles* are men. Kids are... well, they're kids. Had Kevin, at his eighteenth birthday, started to think of himself as a man?

I wondered if the other five dead men were really five more dead kids. I wondered if these same two army men had to deliver the news to five other families. Then I wondered how old *they* were. Their practically shaved heads, and those stupid dress-uniform hats worn so low on their brows, and their I-am-a-rock expressions probably made them look older than they were. Were they eighteen, too? Were they brand-new army guys, just out of boot camp, and was that why they were still here in the United States? Would they be leaving for Vietnam soon themselves, and were they—all the while they were speaking so politely but emotionlessly with us—mentally repeating to themselves: *Not me, not my family; please, God, don't let this happen to me?*

It's not fair, I thought. *It's not fair that it happened to Kevin.*

The army guys' shaved heads made me think of those pictures we had snuck a peek at all those years ago—me and Dwight—Uncle Jack's pictures of the concentration-camp Jews. Americans were supposed to be the good guys. Americans were supposed to win.

But I'd seen enough war movies to know that sometimes the new young guy got killed, especially if he was showing off pictures of the family or the sweetheart back home. Kevin hadn't been foolish enough to be showing pictures of us, had he—or of Millicent Oschmann, whom he'd taken to the senior ball?

These are awfully stupid thoughts, I told myself, *for someone who's just been told her brother is dead.*

I tried to concentrate on what the army guys were saying, but my mind drifted back to World War II again. I remembered the man my father had had to shoot—the wounded one. I wondered if two army guys had shown up on his doorstep, with a telegram for his family.

"My son didn't want to go," Dad told these two army men, these strangers. "It was different in 1942. But I wouldn't listen."

"People got killed, even in 1942," one of them said.

"Yes," Mom whispered so fervently I was sure there was a story there that I had never been told.

Mom was the one who ended up calling Uncle Bud and Uncle Jack to tell them what had happened.

Dad just wandered from room to room, or he'd arrange and rearrange meaningless things, like the pictures of us on the mantel—our formal school portraits, the snapshot he had taken of Kevin and Millicent Oschmann on their way to the senior ball. "It's just...," Dad would start, over and over, then he would shake his head, never finishing.

Mom was the one who selected DiVincenzo's Funeral Parlor and made the arrangements for Kevin's body to be picked up from the airport, and for the funeral service, and for everyone to come back to our house for a meal afterward. She snapped at Aunt Ida and Aunt Lise every time they tried to do what Mom estimated was something *she* was supposed to handle. Dad stayed out of her way. Maybe she would have accepted help from me, but I didn't know what to do, and seeing her bite off Aunt Ida's head once was enough to warn me off.

The only time Mom lost it was when Mr. DiVincenzo refused to open the casket. "You don't understand," she told him. "This is my son. He died in Vietnam. I haven't seen him since he left three months ago."

"I *do* understand," Mr. DiVincenzo said in that professional voice of his that never seemed stressed or flustered. "But the casket has been sealed."

"Unseal it," Mom told him, obviously on the edge of adding something along the lines of *you big, dumb fool.*

But Mr. DiVincenzo was shaking his head, and he told her, "That can't be done."

"Maggie," Dad said.

Mom ignored him. "Is it soldered?" she asked in a voice that from me she would have called sarcastic.

Mr. DiVincenzo didn't take offense at her tone. "Please," he said reasonably. He hesitated, but obviously he wasn't convincing her with gentle stubbornness. "The body is prepared differently if there's going to be an open casket. That hasn't been done."

I could see Mom forcing herself to be reasonable. "Well, have them do it now." She shrugged off the hand Aunt Lise tried to set on her shoulder.

"It can't be done now," Mr. DiVincenzo said. "Please try to understand."

"I *don't* understand. It doesn't make any difference. It's just for the family. You can close it again before the general viewing." She saw Mr. DiVincenzo's glance in my direction. "For me alone, then. I need to say good-bye."

I looked at Dad to see why he didn't say anything. I could see why from his face. I hated my mother at that moment because I knew she was backing Mr. DiVincenzo into a corner from which he'd have to say what Dad and I guessed but didn't want to hear spoken: that Kevin's body wasn't fit to be seen.

Aunt Lise put her arm around my mother's waist. "It's better this way, Maggie," she said. "Remember him the way he was."

"That's easy for you to say," Mom snapped at her, jerking away. "Try to imagine how you'd feel if it were Dwight."

I cringed from the savagery of her words, but Aunt Lise only answered, with a calm certainty which reminded me she had lived through a war in her own homeland, "I would still feel the same."

Mom began to cry. "We don't even know for sure if it's him," she protested. "Mistakes can be made. How can we know?"

My father swore and walked out of the funeral parlor.

Don't leave me, I thought.

But he already had.

Aunt Ida told me, "I need some air. Walk outside with me?"

Aunt Ida was, of course, as sturdy and steady as always. But being a coward, I played along so that I could get out of there.

We were just in time to see Dad's car tearing out of the parking lot, Uncle Jack in the passenger seat, clutching the dashboard for dear life.

By the time we came back in, Mom had settled down.

Of course, Aunt Ida timed our return to coincide with the arrival of other people besides the immediate family, so that might have had something to do with Mom's improved demeanor.

Dad came back shortly afterward. I overheard Uncle Jack telling Uncle Bud that they had had a couple beers to "take the edge off." I saw Mom's disapproving expression, but I don't know if that was for the beers or for leaving her to cope with Mr. DiVincenzo on her own.

Dwight sat next to me and behaved himself as well as a thirteen-year-old boy can—until he told about the time he had gone camping with our family and how Kevin, using the bushes as a bathroom, had sat down in poison ivy.

As soon as the people Dwight had been talking to had moved on, I hissed at him, "That's not the kind of thing to be telling at a funeral."

"Why not?" Dwight asked. "It was funny. It defined the *whole* camping experience for me. Kevin thought it was funny, too, by the next year."

The people he had told the story to were talking to another couple and laughing, though discreetly. I wasn't sure how I felt about people laughing at Kevin's funeral. But the more I thought about it, the more I thought Kevin would have approved.

Which made me cry.

But when I got over that, I decided that I needed to

tell people funny stories about Kevin, too. Still, I left the poison-ivy bathroom incident for Dwight.

There were two afternoons and two evenings at the funeral parlor—and Dad had a couple beers before each of them. He had a beer before the funeral, too, which was at ten o'clock in the morning. Mom grumbled at him that it was getting so you could smell the beer on his breath. Dad just shrugged.

At the cemetery they didn't lower Kevin into the ground while we were watching. From TV I thought they'd do that, and we'd have to throw handfuls of dirt onto the coffin, and the headstone would already be there with his name and the date he had died. I'm not sure I could have handled that. But the headstone wouldn't be ready for a couple months, and after Father Boyle gave the blessing, we were told that we should all go home. Mom started to argue, and Dad told her to just get in the car. They bickered all the way home, but at least they stopped then, not wanting to snarl at each other in front of guests.

I was feeling miserable, wishing everybody would leave, wondering what was the matter with them—expecting us to entertain them when Kevin was dead. And yet I was also dreading when we would be alone, just the three of us, our redefined family unit.

But when everybody left, even the aunts and uncles,

my parents didn't resume their quarreling. Instead Mom went to bed, though it was only one o'clock in the afternoon, and Dad sat on the couch and drank beer after beer. I took pity on Spartacus, whom Dad had ignored ever since we'd gotten the news about Kevin, so I took him for a walk around the block, even though he was a stupid, disgusting dog instead of a beautiful, elegant cat like the one Mary Beth Hinkle had. I think Dad had bought Spartacus for when Kevin came back home, because Kevin had always wanted a dog. *Welcome home, Kevin. We know you did a good job and we're proud of you.*

Anyway, it was hard work walking Spartacus, because his brain was too small to grasp the concepts of *heel* or *no* or *keep away from that lady's flower garden while she's sitting right there on her porch watching, you dimwit dog, you.*

When we finally got back home, Mom was in the living room, wearing only her nightie. It wasn't like her to be downstairs without a robe while the drapes were open so that anybody looking in the window would be able to see her. Not that I think the neighbors were necessarily lining up to try to catch a glimpse of my mother in her nightclothes, but that was one of her idiosyncrasies. Whatever had happened, she had come downstairs fast.

I was concentrating on trying to unfasten Spartacus's leash from his collar. He was twisting and whining and being generally uncooperative. Same as always. Once I got him loose, he tore off into the kitchen as though someone had booted him. Inbred, brain-damaged animal. It was only when I noticed the total silence and looked up to see both my parents watching me that I realized that— up until the moment I'd walked in—their voices had been raised. "What?" I asked.

"Nothing," Dad said.

Mom snorted.

"I fell asleep on the couch," Dad explained. "I had a stupid little nightmare, that's all."

"You were in a drunken stupor," Mom spat out.

"Maggie," Dad protested, with a sidelong glance at me.

"Oh," Mom said, "not in front of Sarah, huh? It would have been nice if you'd shown me the same consideration."

"What?" I repeated.

"I...," Dad began, drawing the word out. Perhaps he sensed that if he didn't say it, Mom would, so he finished, "...thought I saw Kevin."

I remembered Mom asking in the funeral parlor: How would we know if someone had made a mistake and it wasn't really Kevin that was dead? I almost glanced around the room. But they wouldn't have been standing around squabbling if somebody had discovered the error and sent Kevin back here to reassure us.

"How do you think it felt," Mom asked, "to be wakened from a sound sleep with you yelling, 'Kevin! Kevin!'?"

"I wasn't *planning* on waking you and *bothering* you,"

Dad said. "It was a nightmare. Nightmares don't make sense."

"Seeing Kevin was a nightmare?" I asked.

Dad hesitated before explaining, "He was dead. He was dead and he came back."

"Don't drink so much," Mom yelled at him, and she stomped out of the room. A moment later she came back to the doorway to add, "And don't bother coming to our room until you've sobered up!"

"Yeah, yeah," Dad muttered.

And Mary Beth Hinkle wasn't due back for another week.

When it got to be later, I snacked on some of the food people had brought over for us, more for something to do than because I was hungry. Dad ate, too, standing in front of the refrigerator with the door open, eating directly from the Tupperware containers, something he wouldn't have dared if Mom had been there to see. Mom didn't come down at all.

Dad didn't drink any more that afternoon, at least not while I was watching. But he didn't show any sign of going up to join my mother in their bedroom. He seemed to be camped out on the davenport on the porch, as though fascinated by what was going on on our street— even though what was going on was nothing.

I fell asleep on the couch in the living room, in front of the TV, which under normal circumstances my parents wouldn't have allowed. I half woke up when the "Star Spangled Banner" played at the end of the broadcast day—about 2 A.M.—but I didn't have the energy to get up and turn it off, much less climb the stairs to my room. I was just drifting off to the white static from the TV screen when I became aware of a sound that at first I thought was Spartacus whining to get out. But then I heard a sound that *definitely* was Spartacus whimpering, and that was coming from the kitchen, which, after all, was where we kept him at night. This other sound came from the porch.

"Daddy?" I called softly.

My father mumbled something in his sleep. But it didn't sound as though it was in answer to me, because his voice was garbled and agitated.

"Daddy?" I repeated a little louder. But I didn't want to disturb my mother. Especially if my father was having another nightmare. She'd been so sympathetic that afternoon.

"No!" Dad said sharply. But he was still asleep, because whatever he said next was mumbled. Then, more clearly, he shouted, "Keep away!"

Much more of that, and the neighbors would be in on this. Mom would never forgive that. I got up and went to the doorway. "Daddy?" I called into the porch. The moon was down, and since our house was right at the farthest spot between two street lamps, the porch was pretty dark. I could make out the davenport, and the shape of Dad lying on it, tossing as though trying to wake himself up.

I could have gone in and shaken him, but I couldn't bring myself to step into the darkness. I stayed in the doorway and called sharply, "Daddy!"

My father sat up, but then he kind of shrank into one corner of the cushions, cringing, and he said, "Kevin."

From the kitchen, Spartacus started barking.

"Kevin isn't here, Daddy," I said, annoyed with him, annoyed with Spartacus, annoyed with Kevin, for that matter.

"Can't you see him?" my father whispered.

He sure sounded totally awake now. Goose bumps ran up my arms, like icy spiders.

I followed the angle of my father's head. He seemed to be looking into the corner of the porch that was opposite the outside door. There was a shadow from the maple tree, which made it the darkest corner of the porch. It was too dark to really see anything, but I said, "No."

"Get the light," Dad told me.

Now, while I didn't believe Kevin was on the porch, I *didn't* feel like stepping out into the porch, which I would have had to do to get to the light switch. Surely Dad was talking enough to prove that he was awake. So if he was awake, why was he still seeing Kevin?

Was something in that corner?

"Kevin wouldn't hurt you," Dad assured me.

Then why was *he* afraid?

My father was never afraid. He had fought in the war.

He would go after bees that had gotten into the house. He had been the one to calm my mother when the doctor had said that the spot on his lung—which had turned out to be an X-ray technician's error—might be cancer.

I saw an upstairs light go on at the Canettis', across the street, probably in reaction to Spartacus's barking, which had gotten louder and more insistent. I used that as an excuse. I stepped back into the living room. "Spartacus! Hush!" I hissed at the closed kitchen door. Spartacus paused for a moment, then resumed barking. I turned on the living room light, which overflowed into the porch.

When I got back to the doorway that opened on to the porch, Dad had gotten up and turned on the porch light himself. There was nobody else on the porch. In the corner in which we'd been looking was an old porch chair on gliders, and thrown over the back was a sweater that I had left there a couple weeks ago, when the nights had been cooler. Maybe, in the shadows, that had looked like a person sitting there.

"He was here," Dad said. "Sitting here, watching me."

I thought for several long moments before I said, "He's not here now," the most reassuring thing I could come up with.

"He was here," Dad repeated, a whisper barely louder than a sigh....

A whisper that I could hear perfectly well in the silence, since Spartacus had suddenly stopped barking.

"He was here and he's just waiting for me to fall asleep."

And I couldn't think of anything reassuring at all to say to that.

To him or to me.

Dad stayed up the rest of the night, with all the lights on, the way a kid afraid of the dark might.

Still, by the next night, Mom and Dad had made up—or pretended to for my sake—and they went to bed together.

I was awakened about three o'clock by my father's yelling and my mother's crying. I got out of bed and went down the hall to their room.

"How could you *not* have seen him?" Dad was demanding. "He was looming right over me in bed."

I stood in the doorway, thinking that he hadn't had anything to drink all day. That was why Mom had let him back in the bedroom.

"He was not there," Mom sobbed.

"He came out of the shadow in that corner—" Dad started.

"It was a *dream*," my mother insisted.

"It started as a dream, but then I woke up and he was still there."

"Mommy, Daddy," I said, hoping that if they saw me, they would stop fighting. When I had been little, if I had a nightmare my father would say, "Dream or real, I'll protect you," and he would sit by my bed until I fell back to sleep. If I said that now, would Dad feel safe, or would he think I was mocking him? I would protect him if I could.

"Sarah, please," Mom said, "can you get that dog of yours to stop barking before the neighbors complain?"

My dog? All of a sudden, Spartacus was my dog?

But I went down to the kitchen to see what I could do about calming him. I gave him a Milk-Bone, figuring he was the kind of dog who might get distracted by a treat the way—sometimes—I can be distracted by chocolate. I was right. He forgot whatever he'd heard or smelled in the night and scarfed down the Milk-Bone.

On my way out of the kitchen, I met my father, coming downstairs with a pillow. He didn't meet my eyes as he settled down on the couch. "Good night," he told me.

"Good night," I said, but he had a book with him. Pillow or no pillow, it was obvious he wasn't planning on going to sleep.

"Leave the hall light on," he said as I went upstairs. I left the hall light on.

The next morning I was still in bed, vaguely aware of my father showering, getting ready for work. This would be his first day back at the tool-and-die shop since we'd gotten the news about Kevin. I could smell the coffee my mother was brewing in the kitchen and could hear Spartacus scratching at the kitchen door to get out.

Nice, normal sounds from a nice, normal household.

I was just about to drift back to sleep when I heard my father scream. It was worse than when he'd yelled in his sleep, for this was a scream of pain.

I fought with the sheet that had gotten tangled around my legs, and heard Mom running up the stairs. I almost collided with her in the hall outside the bathroom. She gave me a look that was too complicated for me to read, and tore the door open.

Dad was backed up against the wall, wildly swinging his razor as though to keep someone away from him. Half his face was still lathered; on the other side there was a long cut that more or less followed his jawbone, and blood dripped onto his white T-shirt. "He tried to grab my hand," Dad shouted. Now he sounded more angry than frightened or hurt. "He tried to make me cut my own throat."

"He didn't!" Mom screamed at him. "Even if Kevin *did* come back from the dead, he would never do that! Where is he? *Where?* I don't see him. Sarah doesn't see him. You're imagining this!"

"He wants me dead," Dad said. He held a towel to the cut to staunch the bleeding. But in the meanwhile he didn't put down the razor.

"How can you say that?" Mom screamed at him. "How can you say that about Kevin?"

"Should I call an ambulance?" I asked.

"I am *not* hallucinating!" my father shouted at me.

I had meant for the cut—though the bleeding was

slowing down, not nearly as bad as I had feared when I'd first walked in. His words played in my head. So did others. Those amusing little comments from cartoons: sending for the men in the little white coats, calling the guys from the funny farm. Not for my father.

Not for my father.

Mom said, "You need to talk to someone about this, Tom. Dreaming is one thing—"

"These have not been dreams," Dad insisted.

"You're destroying what's left of this family." Mom pushed past me and fled the room, sobbing. Dad, still holding that razor, took a step toward the door. I wanted to yell, "Run, Mom!" to warn her.

But Dad only threw the razor in the trash.

How could I have thought—even for an instant—that he would harm her?

"I won't let him get me," Dad muttered.

I felt guilty that I was so glad when Dad left for work. But I was still glad.

Then he came home from his job midafternoon, which was about two hours too early. Dread sat in the pit of my stomach as I watched him come up the walk.

"He followed me," Dad said.

Not in the dark of night. Not when waking up from a nightmare. Not when he needed someone to blame for cutting himself.

"Oh, Tom," Mom said, between pity and exasperation.

"There're too many machines," he said. "The drill press. Tumbler. Grinder. Lathe. All it would take would be one moment of inattention, and he could come up behind me, and that would be the end of me."

"Kevin wouldn't do that," I protested, as though rational protests could convince him.

Dad looked at me with a level, evaluating expression. "Not before," he agreed. "But now that he's dead..." He nodded to show he understood that Kevin's death had changed things. "He's just waiting, hiding in the shadows, waiting for his chance."

His words obviously scared my mother as much as they were scaring me.

"You haven't slept properly in days," she said. "That's what's causing this. Let me call Dr. Farrell to see if he can give you a prescription to help you sleep and you'll see—"

"No!" Dad cried as though shocked that Mom could be so stupid. "I have to keep my wits." Dad sat rocking on the chair that wasn't a rocking chair. "Can't let Kevin get the drop on me. He's getting stronger. Every time he comes, he's getting stronger." The scabbed-over cut on his left cheek and the stubble on his right from when he had given up shaving midway through gave him an alarming appearance, like some of the spookier hippies protesting at the colleges.

Don't do this! I wanted to yell at him.

"Fine," Mom said sharply. "I'll start dinner."

But she must really have gone into the kitchen to use the phone, for Uncle Jack and Aunt Lise showed up within a half hour, standing on the stoop, knocking on the door to the porch. Uncle Jack was still wearing his mechanics overalls from the Esso station where he worked. Though he had cleaned his hands, he still had grease on his face. Dwight was with them, wearing a T-shirt that said NIAGARA FALLS MUSEUM OF THE BIZARRE. Talk about appropriate.

"It's the dinner patrol," Uncle Jack announced cheerfully through the screen door. "Lise has declared she's not cooking tonight, and we thought maybe you and Maggie and Sarah needed the night off, too. Our treat. We'll take you all out to dinner."

"We're not dressed," Dad said.

Uncle Jack snorted. "Do we look dressed? It's not like we're offering to take you anyplace *nice*—just the hot-dog stand by the pier."

"That's so kind," Mom said, already untying her apron. "I can just put away what I started and save that for tomorrow. Come on, Tom."

I held my breath. *Please, please, please,* I mentally begged. Uncle Jack was always good at making things better. I was sure his company would be good for my father.

Dad eyed them warily. But, "Let me get my sneakers," he said to my relief. He went upstairs, and Uncle Jack winked at my mother through the screen door.

Everything was going to be all right, I was sure of it.

Then Spartacus, who had let Uncle Jack's car into the driveway without uttering a single guard-doglike sound, who had let Uncle Jack and Aunt Lise onto the stoop, who had let them ring the doorbell, who had let Dwight press his face against the porch screen—not a pleasant sight at all—suddenly started barking.

At first I thought he had finally become aware that we had visitors and was trying to warn them away from his territory. He tore into the porch and lunged at the door, not even giving Aunt Lise, who was closest, time to get properly scared. But he wasn't after her. He just bowled his way between Mom and the door and Aunt Lise, tearing out of the house to the freedom of the outdoors.

"Oh no," I complained, because I was always the one who had to chase him down and try to coax him back home. Try roaming up and down your neighborhood yelling, "Spartacus! Spartacus, come back!" and see if *you* don't feel entirely humiliated.

Maybe, if I was lucky, Uncle Jack would ask Dwight to go. But just then we could hear my father start to come down the stairs into the living room. Then his footsteps stopped. "No!" Dad yelled. "No, Kevin! Keep away! Keep away from me!"

Uncle Jack pushed past me and my mother into the house.

Through the doorway I could see Dad crouched on

the stairs, his arms protectively over his head. There was no sign of anything that could even vaguely be construed as shadowy, much less as Kevin.

Being the coward I am, I went after Spartacus. *Please let my father be all right,* I prayed to the beat of my sneakers pounding the sidewalk.

It took several minutes for me to corner Spartacus and get a firm hold on his collar. When I got back Uncle Jack's car was still in the driveway, but there was no sign of him or Aunt Lise. Dwight was sitting on the stoop, experimenting with how long he could stretch out his bubble gum. By his unhappy expression I guessed he had been ordered to stay outside.

"Hey," he said when he saw me dragging Spartacus up the walk. He stuck the gum back in his mouth even though his hands, which he had been touching it with, were filthy. "He always do that?"

"Do what?" I asked, figuring he meant did my dad always act like his dead son was attacking him. I had no intention of making things easy for Dwight.

But Dwight nodded his head toward Spartacus. "Does Nero there always get wigged out whenever Kevin makes an appearance?"

I could have strangled the little creep. "You are such an insensitive jerk," I told him.

"All right, all right; *Spartacus,*" Dwight corrected, as though I was mad because he'd gotten the dog's name wrong, when he was always calling him Tiberius or Claudius or something. "Don't be so sensitive. *He* doesn't know what his name is."

I would have smacked Dwight, but I didn't dare let go of Spartacus's collar. He wasn't quite so wiggly as before, but I didn't have the stamina to chase him three blocks again.

"Kevin is dead," I told Dwight, as though he needed reminding. "My father..."—I took a long, shuddery breath and said it out loud for the first time—"my father is going crazy." *Nutty as a fruitcake. Got bats in the belfry. Not playing with a full deck. One can short of a six-pack.* The airy words to describe the darkness in my father's head played in *my* head. Angrily I finished, "And that's nothing to make jokes about."

"I'm not," Dwight protested.

"Would you just get the door and shut up."

Dwight opened the door to the porch, and I pushed Spartacus in. Spartacus jumped up onto the davenport as though he had never even *heard* of the outside world, much less tried to escape into it. Worn-out from his exertions, he laid his head on his paws.

I could hear Uncle Jack's voice, and my father's, coming from the living room. I didn't want to go in, so I curled up next to Spartacus, who was stinky, but at least he was soft.

Dwight had obviously been given strict instructions

that he was *not* to come in. He pressed his face against the screen again. "Hey," he called to me from the stoop. "Hey, Sarah."

"Go away." I buried my face into Spartacus's furry shoulder.

"Uncle Tom sees Kevin?" Dwight asked. When I didn't answer, he asked, "And you and Aunt Maggie don't?" And when I still didn't answer, he asked, "But the dog does?"

"*The dog doesn't see Kevin*," I said between clenched teeth.

"Does he always act weird when your father is seeing him?"

"He *always* acts weird," I said. "He has a brain the size of a pea."

"Dogs can sense things people can't," Dwight said. "Like those whistles that are too high-pitched for humans to hear."

"You're saying Kevin has come back from the dead to blow a dog whistle at Spartacus?" Dwight could be such a moron.

"Stop acting so damn superior," Dwight told me.

I thought about what he was saying. "My dad is acting weird. He jumps up and he yells and he moves fast. *That's* what's spooking the dog."

"Your father was upstairs when the dog got spooked," Dwight pointed out. "Spartacus was in the living room;

he saw something that made him want to get away. *Then* your father came down and saw what Spartacus saw: Kevin." He was looking very pleased with himself.

I straightened up. "There's no such thing as ghosts."

Dwight held his arms out in a hey-don't-blame-me gesture.

"And even," I said, *"even* if there were, Kevin would *not* do the things my dad thinks he's doing. He wouldn't threaten him. He wouldn't be trying to hurt him. Kevin..." I sighed. "Kevin was never like that."

Dwight sat down on the stoop. "No," he agreed. "But something is going on. Sure, your father is sad that Kevin died. But is that enough to make him see things that aren't there? Let me help you investigate this."

"I'm not—" I started, but just then my mother and Uncle Jack and Aunt Lise came out. Mom looked angry; I think she was embarrassed, and that made her angry. Uncle Jack looked shaken. Aunt Lise rested her cheek against mine. She probably wouldn't have done that if she'd been aware that until a minute ago my cheek had been against the dog, but it was a nice gesture. "Everything is going to be fine," she assured me. "Jack has gotten your father to agree to see a doctor tomorrow."

Tomorrow he might change his mind, I thought.

She finished: "He thinks a quiet night at home would be best for this evening. We'll go out to dinner tomorrow, okay? All of us."

I nodded. What else could I do? *Demand* that they take me out?

Dwight asked, "Can I spend the night?"

"No." Aunt Lise didn't even glance at my mother to see if it was okay with her.

"But—"

"Move," Uncle Jack commanded.

Dwight moved. But so did my mother. She accompanied my aunt and uncle out of the porch and down the three steps of the stoop. They stood by the car, talking, their voices quiet, their faces earnest. Dwight took the opportunity to press his face once more against the screen door. "Remember," he whispered, "take your cue from the dog."

Yeah, right. Compared to Dwight, the dog almost *did* seem smart.

Could Spartacus see something that none of the rest of us could, except Dad?

And if there was something to see, what else could it be but Kevin?

Was I stubbornly refusing to believe Dwight could be right, just because he was Dwight?

"So what do you think is going on?" I asked. "Not all dead people come back as ghosts, or Gramma Cassie would still be hanging around family picnics, force-feeding us those rock-solid diabetic cookies of hers. So why has Kevin come back?"

"Unsettled business," Dwight said. "That's why ghosts

get tied to Earth. Wrongs to be righted, that sort of thing." He had a question of his own: "Why does your father think Kevin is here?"

"To...I don't know..." It sounded so stupid. "To get him."

"Why?"

Exasperated, I said, "I thought we already agreed Kevin wouldn't be that way."

"But why would your father *think* he would? Did your father used to beat him, or anything like that, that he thinks Kevin could want revenge for?"

"No," I said.

The thing I remembered was that picture of Kevin and Millicent Oschmann on prom night—how they'd had to wait for Dad, who had run off to the store for flash cubes for the camera, then everybody smiling and waving, everybody thinking we had forever.

Dwight sat on the stoop; I sat on the other side of the door in the porch—both of us resting our chins on our hands, thinking.

"They used to get along," I said, "until..." And there it was: the solution Dwight was looking for. "Dad's feeling guilty," I said, "for supporting the war, for encouraging Kevin"—that wasn't it by half—"for bullying him into serving instead of running off to Canada. *It was different,* I remembered him saying, *but I wouldn't listen.* I finished: "He thinks he's responsible for Kevin being dead."

"But," Dwight said, "what's really happening is that Kevin keeps coming back—not because he *wants* to, but because your father himself keeps *calling* him back by his own feelings of guilt." Dwight saw the skeptical look on my face. "It's a possibility," he said.

So is intelligent life on Mars.

But I liked Dwight's interpretation a lot better than my father's. Or mine.

"Dwight," I started.

But I never finished.

There was a sound from the house.

And just as Mom, Dad, and I had known Kevin was dead as soon as we'd seen those army guys, so, too, we all immediately recognized the significance of that sound: It was a gun. I knew that without even having known my father had a gun—a Luger, I was told later, a German officer's gun, a memento that lots of World War II veterans brought home with them. But in that single moment after the shot, I saw Aunt Lise flinch, Uncle Jack whirl back toward the house, Mom sway and catch hold of the car door. Dwight's eyes looked ready to bug out of his head. Spartacus began to whimper. As for me, I was just empty. Perhaps I had finally figured it out; perhaps not. Perhaps there would have been something I could have done with the knowledge I thought I had. Perhaps not. In that moment, I knew I would never know.

What happened to my father inside the house while

the rest of us were all outside discussing him? Did he intentionally shoot himself from grief or guilt? Did he *accidentally* shoot himself while trying to protect himself from Kevin? *Was* Kevin's ghost there—and if so, did he return specifically to try to stop Dad from killing himself? Or am I wrong about Kevin? Did he set out to drive our father to his death? Can a ghost be angry enough, and substantial enough, to aim a gun and pull a trigger? Were we blockheads to base so much of our theory on the behavior of a brain-damaged dog?

"Stay here," Uncle Jack commanded us—me and Dwight, though neither of us had twitched—as he yanked the porch door open and ran into the house. Aunt Lise was holding my mother. Dwight and I were staring at each other. Spartacus took the opportunity to run through the open door into the front yard, where he stood and bayed at the sky.

When the Canettis peeked out their window to see what the problem was, I finally took Spartacus by the collar and told him, "That's enough."

And he stopped.

The Ghost

When Jessica screamed, Mark and Adam came running so fast, they nearly bowled me over.

"Did you see it?" she yelled. "Did you see that thing?"

We all peered around the room and shook our heads.

"It was terrible!" she said. "I've never seen anything like it."

Adam took a deep breath before speaking. While Jessica and I had been inside, he and Mark had been struggling to get the refrigerator up the front stairs, and his patience had obviously been left behind. "If it was a bug," he warned, "or a mouse—"

"Bug!" she shouted. Her chest heaved under the tight T-shirt, which boldly proclaimed, ARCHAEOLOGISTS DIG IT—SUNY COLLEGE AT OSWEGO. She had been working hard, also. The previous occupants, gone two years now, had left their furniture behind, and she had been cleaning the large, dusty rooms and trying to arrange the

111

new and the old furniture so everything fit. That must be a girl thing, wanting everything to be perfectly right from the very beginning. Her exertions and her recent scare made her voice strained. "Mouse? What kind of jerk do you think I am? It was a person. A horrible, disgusting, slimy, half-human *person*."

"'Disgusting'?" I said. "'*Slimy*'?"

Mark also seemed incredulous. "'Half human'?"

Adam started for the window.

"No, right here in the house," Jessica said. "He was standing there all *dripping* and ... and ... foul, and *leering* at me. And then he just kind of dissolved into thin air."

Leering was just like her; she was the type who'd always suspect a guy's ulterior motives—even a slimy, disgusting, half-human guy.

Mark seemed to have the same idea. "'*Leering*,' Jessica?"

"Where, exactly, was this thing?" Adam asked, trying to take charge.

"There, right there." She pointed to where I stood, and I had to move quickly to get out of Adam's way.

He crouched down, examined the dust patterns. He had already finished sophomore year in archaeology and obviously felt his training qualified him as some sort of forensic expert.

"Any slime there?" I asked. "Any drips?"

"Well, see anything?" Mark interrupted. "Any cloven hoof tracks or whatever?"

"Cute, Mark, real cute," Jessica snapped.

Adam stood up. "Well, of course, there's all the tracks we've made moving our stuff in here, but I don't see anything that looks out of order. Tell you what: Why don't you sit down and rest for a while, Jessica?"

"Don't take that tone with me."

"'Tone'? What *tone*?" Adam was a bit too defensive. "That was concern you detected in my voice."

"Bull. That was a Jessica's-been-seeing-things-that-aren't-there–Must-be-that-time-of-month tone."

"Come on, Jess."

I was biting my cheeks over this exchange, and one look at Mark showed he was enjoying himself, also. Not that I knew him that well, but I thought we had a lot in common. If it weren't for those other two! They were only interested in this fine old house because the real-estate broker was willing to rent it out cheap to college students until a buyer turned up. There was no way the four of us could share the house in peace.

"You think I'm just imagining things," Jessica was accusing. "That I believed Donna Horvath's stories and got carried away with my own daydreams."

"Of course not," Adam said so quickly that we all knew that was exactly what he was thinking.

"Big deal," Jessica said. "So a murder was committed in this house. That doesn't bother me."

"Here," I said, "in this room."

"Right here," Mark echoed.

"As the poor guy dozed in this very rocking chair," I finished, "his dear brother beat him to death for the sake of a woman who didn't really love either of them."

As if on cue, all of us turned from the antique rocker and looked at the fireplace, but of course the police had kept the poker as evidence.

"And we know that the murderer confessed but then hung himself in his jail cell before telling what he'd done with the body," Jessica continued. "As for the rest of it, that's just garbage: how the dead guy came back and *haunted* his brother, brandishing the murder weapon—the fireplace poker—until the brother turned himself in. How the ghost followed him to jail and drove him to suicide. I never gave the story a second thought."

"Until now," I said.

"Until now," she echoed. She rubbed her arms. "Jeez, this place is depressing. I think we made a mistake renting it."

"It's better than the dorms," Adam started.

"I think we need some air," I said. I could see what was coming, but I couldn't help myself. With perfect timing I threw the window up just as an owl hooted.

Jessica, as could be counted on, overreacted and screamed.

"There, there," I whispered just loud enough for her to hear, then patted her on the back. The more I patted, the more she screamed.

Finally I pulled a hanky out of Adam's pocket and fanned her with it. Jessica started hyperventilating.

"That does it," Adam said. "Let's get out of here."

It had taken them about three hours to unload their stuff, but they got it all back in the truck in less than thirty minutes.

"Good-bye," I called as they piled themselves in.

I wanted someone to stay—really I did. Otherwise, I'd never rest properly. But I found it hard to resist playing my little jokes.

I watched the truck pull out of the driveway, then went back into the house and sat down in the old oak rocker—always my favorite, despite what had happened to me there. Perhaps later I would go visit my special place in the lower garden.

For Love of Him

It was no good trying to outrun the rain. Harrison realized that after those few frantic seconds when the first big drops pelted the leaves in the uppermost branches, hard enough to be audible. Already soaked, he wasn't running, for the roads in the old section of the cemetery could be treacherously slippery. He was caught, naturally, just about halfway between the cemetery office, where the rest rooms were, and the area where his troop was helping Allan earn his Eagle Badge by cleaning up litter and debris from around the graves.

He almost missed seeing the woman kneeling by a grave not far from the road. It was only the near-simultaneous flash of lightning and crack of thunder that caused him to jerk his head up, into the eye-stinging rain. For a moment he thought he was seeing mist, a product of the combination of hot spring day and cold rain.

As soon as he saw it was a woman in a white dress,

Harrison stopped looking, reluctant to intrude on someone's privacy, even if that person was unaware of him.

But then he glanced back.

The woman just knelt there as though oblivious to Harrison, to the pouring rain, to the danger of a thunderstorm with all these centuries-old trees around. She rocked back and forth, her pale hands covering her face. Her white dress and her long dark hair were plastered to her body, giving her the look of a black-and-white photograph. Even from the road Harrison could see her shoulders shaking.

Strange, he thought, that anybody should be so overcome by grief here in the old part of the cemetery. Most of these graves dated back to the 1800s, which was why this section looked so like a park: The Victorians had had a weird perspective on things. These days sightseers came here to take pictures of the grand angels or to make rubbings of the stones with their elaborate carvings and their flowery testimonials.

Why such heartfelt tears for someone at least a hundred years dead?

Harrison glimpsed Mr. Reisinger's van rounding the hill on the lower road. "Mr. R.!" he called, waving his arms, though with the rain and thunder and distance, the scoutmaster couldn't possibly hear.

But he must have been on the lookout for Harrison. He flashed his headlights to show he'd spotted him.

Harrison watched the van make its way around the pond, when he remembered the woman. Should he offer her a ride? But the woman was no longer there. *Silly*, Harrison thought. You'd think she'd come to the road on a day like this, rather than cut across the back way to the old buggy path. But perhaps she'd been embarrassed to have been caught at... whatever.

Harrison stepped onto the rain-slicked grass. "Miss?" he called over the surly rumbling of thunder. The sheet of rain prevented him from seeing far at all. He thought he caught a glimpse of a figure beyond the willow tree, but that seemed to be a man, a tall, thin, dark-haired man. And then he was gone, too.

"Miss?"

Harrison took another step. He heard the crunch of gravel as the van approached on the road behind him. "Do you want a ride?" he called. "You shouldn't be out here during a lightning storm."

There was no answer, but by then Harrison was almost to the grave by which the woman had been kneeling. He took the few extra steps.

It was a double headstone. ROBERT DELANO ADAMS was inscribed on one side.

LOVING SON
LONG WILL HE BE REMEMBERED
LONG WILL HE BE MISSED
HIS MOTHER GRIEVES STILL
JANUARY 10, 1874–MAY 17, 1892

A hundred years ago today. What an odd coincidence. He did the mental arithmetic. Only a few years older than himself.

The other side bore the name EULALIA MEINYK. There was only one date, two days later than the other: MAY 19, 1892.

SHE DIED FOR LOVE OF HIM

How very sad, Harrison thought.

Mr. Reisinger beeped the horn, calling him back to here and now, and motioned for him to get moving.

He clambered in next to Spense, who made a face at Harrison for dripping on him.

"Don't know enough to come in out of the rain," Mr. Reisinger said over the noise of the windshield wipers. He shook his head, then reached under the seat and pulled out a roll of paper towels, which he passed back.

"We get enough done?" Harrison asked.

Mr. Reisinger was a professional gardener who had contracts to take care of several dozen of the newer graves, so he'd be very fussy about the cleanup the scouts had done. But he said, "Probably," and Harrison leaned back in his seat.

"You smell like a wet dog," Spense complained, friendly as always.

Harrison gazed out the window as they approached the stone-and-iron gate. How pretty the trees looked, their leaves still fresh and new, the trunks and branches stained dark by the rain, with the dramatically gray clouds as backdrop. Robert Delano Adams and Eulalia Meinyk. He wondered which one the woman had been crying for.

The next day, Monday, Harrison was riding his bike home from school and decided to cut through the cemetery. *We did a good job,* he told himself, but then he rounded a corner and saw that somebody had lopped the heads off all the tulips Mr. Reisinger had planted over Mrs. Reisinger's grave. In fact, for the entire length of this row, wreaths were knocked off their stands, ivy and geraniums were trampled. When Harrison got off the bike and walked around to the other side, he saw that someone had used a red felt-tip marker to deface the fronts of the headstones. A few had obscene messages scrawled on them, but many simply had a line drawn through the names, as though the vandals had simply held the marker out when they strolled past.

Stupid, senseless malice. And this was just the kind of thing Mr. Reisinger had complained the police were useless for. They'd take the report—they always took a report—but they weren't interested unless there was dramatic breakage. Angrily Harrison got out the linen handkerchief his mother always tucked into his backpack and spat on it. On his knees he scrubbed at Mrs. Reisinger's headstone—one of the ones that was simply scribbled on. The ink came off the smooth surface easily, but he had to scrape it out of the engraved areas of the letters.

Finished, he sat back on his heels. On the grave to the left, someone had covered the inscription MOTHER with a particularly crude word. The grave was not one of the ones Mr. Reisinger was responsible for, but it was a recent grave and had been well tended. Now the urn with fresh flowers was overturned. Harrison could just picture this poor woman's husband and children coming with some new flowers this weekend and seeing that obscenity. With a sigh he began scrubbing at the word.

Three hours later he'd scrubbed clean all the gravestones with actual words on them. The knees of his school pants were filthy, and his hands were too sore to do any more. *Sorry,* he thought to the others.

The scents of crushed flowers and damp earth heated by the sun mingled and hung heavily about him. *What is the matter with me?* he thought. He'd just spent all afternoon cleaning gravestones for people he didn't even know, who wouldn't even be aware of what he'd done, who might not even care. And for what? He was late for dinner, which always made his mother crazy; he'd missed the chance to go to the library to research his science paper, which was due tomorrow; and he still had to pick up a snack for the scout meeting tonight.

Harrison jammed what was left of the handkerchief into his pocket, unsure whether he was more sad or angry.

Somehow, despite all the times he had been here, he missed the turnoff to the exit. He was pedaling past the reconstructed Victorian gazebo before he realized he was in the old section. Rather than backtrack, he kept going. The road circled around, anyway, and came out near the old chapel. There was the grave of abolitionist Frederick Douglass. On the other side of that hill were buried the poor nameless children who had died in the turn-of-the-century orphanage fire. Over there just beyond the curve of the road was the infant son of Wild West showman Buffalo Bill Cody. Instead of going that way, Harrison turned down the road to take him deeper into the cemetery. He slowed down, unsure he'd recognize it, sure he must have passed it already. Then—just as he was about to give up—he spotted it. ROBERT DELANO ADAMS. EULALIA MEINYK.

He left the bike by the road.

What am I doing here? he asked himself. Surely he hadn't expected the strange dark-haired woman to still be here.

He ran his fingers across the cool marble, tracing the outlines of the letters. ROBERT DELANO ADAMS. EULALIA MEINYK. SHE DIED FOR LOVE OF HIM. Two days later. Had she died of a broken heart? People used to do that, back then. What must he have been like for her to be unable to go on without him? Had she taken her own life? SHE DIED FOR LOVE OF HIM.

Without planning it, Harrison sat down next to the grave. *What am I doing here?* he asked himself again.

Just resting, he answered himself. *As soon as I catch my breath, I'll be on my way.*

But the next thing he knew, it was dark out, and Mr. Reisinger was shaking his shoulder.

"What?" he said. "What is it?"

"*'What is it?'*" the scoutmaster repeated. "It's nine o'clock at night, and your parents are frantic. The whole troop and half the neighborhood are out looking for you. What are you doing?"

"I must have fallen asleep," Harrison said. But he was still sitting up, and he knew his eyes had been wide open, though he couldn't remember what he'd been looking at.

The groundskeeper who'd opened the gate for Mr. Reisinger told Harrison to keep out of the cemetery from now on; his parents told him to keep out of the cemetery; the police told him to keep out of the cemetery.

But his science teacher made him stay after school because his report wasn't done, and he didn't want to worry his parents by being late again, so he took the shortcut, anyway.

Everything's fine, he told himself, ignoring the pounding of his heart and the damp feeling around the edge of his scalp. So why were his hands slippery on the handlebars?

He rode past the stone chapel and into the old section, where the trees were tall and the roads wound dizzyingly and the graves seemed scattered randomly in the most improbable places rather than being lined up in neat rows. He was aware that he was breathing with his mouth open, and still he couldn't get enough air. What was the matter with him?

He stopped pedaling, and the bike coasted to a stop. For several minutes he just sat there straddling his bike, staring straight ahead.

A woman and her dog jogged by, the dog's chain collar jangling.

Harrison finally turned his head and faced the double headstone. ROBERT DELANO ADAMS. MAY 17, 1892. EULALIA MEINYK. MAY 19, 1892. SHE DIED FOR LOVE OF HIM. Harrison closed his eyes. SHE DIED FOR LOVE OF HIM.

He left the bike and approached the gravesite. 1874–1892. Robert had been eighteen when he'd died. Of what? And how old had Eulalia been? SHE DIED FOR LOVE OF HIM. A hundred years ago today. Had they been engaged? Was that why they were buried together? If so, she was probably a little bit younger than Robert. Maybe about Harrison's own age, since people back then married young.

Harrison had lived near the cemetery for as long as he could remember, but he'd never thought about dying before, about being dead.

He thought about it now.

He put his hand on the stone and tried to imagine what Robert and Eulalia had been like. It was they who had been here Sunday afternoon, he was sure of it. He had seen pictures of people of the late 1800s skating on the Genesee River—the men in top hats, the women with fur muffs. He imagined Robert and Eulalia skating on the river. Had they come to the cemetery for Sunday picnics, the way the cemetery tour guides said Victorians used to do, sitting perhaps on that hill there, overlooking the pond? Harrison imagined them laughing together, their voices clear as angels' song, so much in love that one couldn't live without the other. SHE DIED FOR LOVE OF HIM. Nobody loved Harrison that much. Nobody ever would.

"Kid?" the breeze seemed to whisper. "Kid?" Then, more insistent, more human, "Are you all right?" Harrison opened his eyes and found that he had somehow ended up kneeling on the ground. He blinked in the bright sunlight. Birds were chirping. In the distance, at the farthest edge of hearing, someone was mowing a lawn. The woman jogger with the dog stood poised on the grass between him and the curb as though unsure how close she should approach. She held on to the dog's collar to keep him from bounding over to Harrison.

"I'm"—his voice sounded so husky and unused—"taking a shortcut home so I won't be late." He ran his tongue over his parched lips.

The jogger hesitated before nodding. "Oh." Her jaw twitched, perhaps an attempt at a smile. She took a step back toward the road.

Harrison pulled himself up by leaning on the gravestone.

The jogger tugged on the chain collar until she and her dog were both on the road. Harrison checked his bicycle's wheels and chain and handlebars and seat while the two of them disappeared over the crest of the hill. Then he got back off and knelt by the grave.

SHE DIED FOR LOVE OF HIM. Harrison didn't think he could bear the incredible sadness of it. That they had lived and loved and died before he had even been born. Before his parents had been born. History had always seemed unreal to him, as though everything that had ever happened in the whole of the world had been leading up to him, to whatever moment he was experiencing. Now he felt unreal. Surely things had peaked here, in 1892, for Robert and Eulalia. Surely *he* was superfluous, extra, unneeded. Not smart. Not loved. Worthless. Nobody would ever grieve at his grave.

We would, a voice whispered into his ear, a voice as warm and beautiful and clear as the singing of angels. *We have enough love left over for you. Come to us. Trust us.*

Harrison lay down on the grass and closed his eyes.

We're the ones who care for you, another gentle voice whispered. *Only we. No one else.*

But then a shadow fell across him, blocking out the sun, so that he shivered. "Hello, Harrison," a quiet voice said.

Harrison looked up and blinked several times to get the tears out of his eyes. Tears for himself. Tears for Robert and Eulalia. They were waiting for him. They'd make everything better.

"Remember me? Charlie Sonneman?"

SHE DIED FOR LOVE OF HIM. Slowly the vision retreated; the voices retreated. That was all right. He'd be able to call them back. "Hello, Mr. Sonneman," Harrison said. This was Mr. Reisinger's partner in the gardening business. Or at least he had been. Vaguely Harrison remembered hearing that Mr. Sonneman had retired last summer for health reasons. Why was he bothering Harrison now?

"How are you doing, Harrison?"

"Fine," Harrison said, still lying flat on his back.

"I was wondering if you could give me a lift to the gatehouse."

Harrison would have thought Mr. Sonneman was too

old for riding double on a bike, but apparently Mr. Sonneman didn't think so. Harrison was annoyed at the interruption, but he figured he could always come back.

"Hasn't your father ever told you," Mr. Sonneman asked as he took hold of the edge of the seat behind Harrison, "not to talk to strangers?"

"You're not a stranger, Mr. Sonneman."

"I'm not talking about me. I'm talking about those two: Robert Adams and Eulalia Meinyk."

Harrison slammed on the brakes hard enough to jerk them both forward.

"Probably you should go home for the rest of the day," Mr. Sonneman said, ignoring the sudden stop, ignoring the expression that must have been on Harrison's face as Harrison turned to stare at him. "Tomorrow will be easier. You'll be out of danger then. Anniversaries are a powerful thing. As are thunderstorms. And hate."

"She died for love of him," Harrison protested.

Mr. Sonneman shrugged. "Robert's mother wrote that. She never would believe anything bad about him. But Eulalia knew. He was a drunk and a cheat. He used to beat her. Eulalia got hold of a revolver, one of those little white-painted, very ladylike jobs they used to make, and blew his head off."

"That can't be true," Harrison protested.

Mr. Sonneman continued as though Harrison hadn't interrupted. "They had promised each other, once, at the beginning, to love each other forever, to the grave and beyond—which was the sort of extravagant thing they used to say back then. Very emotional people, the Victorians. They wove jewelry out of their hair, you know, to be remembered after they died."

"But it says she died for love of him," Harrison insisted. "I saw her." There; he'd said it out loud. "I saw her crying for him."

Mr. Sonneman shook his head. "I've seen her, too. She cries for herself, Harrison. She said she'd love him forever. He held her to that. He waited two days after he died, and then he came for her. They heard her scream, but her door was locked. They had to break it down. They found her strangled. She didn't die for love of him. She died for *promising* to love him.

"The dead can be very jealous, you know, some of them. They get lonely in their graves and come looking for company. They whisper lies in your ears. They feed on your own doubts and weaknesses until there's nothing left of you at all."

"That's an awful thought!"

"Some of them." Mr. Sonneman shrugged. "There are ghosts, and then there are ghosts. You know you're loved, don't you, Harrison? They couldn't fool you with those lies, could they?"

Harrison looked away in shame, thinking of his parents, of his friends—of the uncountable ways they had shown their love for him over the years.

"Sunday was the hundredth anniversary of his death. Today is hers. They'll have less hold on you tomorrow. Even less now, because now you know. They won't be able to manipulate your emotions anymore."

Harrison shuddered, remembering the tears that had stung his eyes, as though they'd occurred a long time ago, to somebody he no longer was.

"I'll get off here," Mr. Sonneman said. "Go home." He patted Harrison's shoulder. "Rest."

Finally he got his mouth to work, but by then Mr. Sonneman had already walked halfway up the hill, where Harrison couldn't follow with the bike, or at least not easily. "Wait."

"Not all the dead are like that," Mr. Sonneman called back.

"But how do you know?..." Too late. He was already gone.

Very strange, Harrison thought.

And thought it again the following week when he started to ask Mr. Reisinger about his old partner Charlie Sonneman and his peculiar view regarding jealous ghosts. Mr. Reisinger only shook his head and told him Charlie had died last fall.

October Chill

The worst part about dying, Emily thought, was knowing it was coming. Which was ridiculous, she knew: *Everyone* would die, eventually. Everyone *knew* it was coming. Eventually.

It was that *eventually* that made all the difference in the world.

Not every sixteen-year-old knew she wouldn't see seventeen. Not everyone had gone through test after painful test only to have her doctor tell her, "From now on, we'll concentrate on keeping you comfortable."

Still, for the moment Emily *was* comfortable. Emily's mother, who always tried to find something positive about everything, pointed out that at least Emily hadn't had to go through chemotherapy and lose her hair. It was hard to find a whole lot of comfort in that, but Emily supposed she should be grateful that she didn't look obviously sick. Because the last thing she wanted was people knowing.

And people didn't know. Except for her family, of course. And the doctor. And the doctor's staff. And the people at the support group her parents had forced her to join. Not that she had any plans to go back *there* if whining and sulking could get her out of it. The only good thing about support group was they had finally convinced her mother that hovering was bad. But in any case, at least she didn't have people on the street giving her that pitying look she'd seen them give to the other kids who went to the same oncologist, with their bald heads, and the circles under their eyes, and their arms all bruised from the injections and the IVs.

See, Emily told herself, *you have a lot to be thankful for.* So far there was no pain, or nothing the medication couldn't handle, anyway. And she still had her hair. And her school friends and her neighbors didn't know about the inoperable tumor growing in her head. And...

Emily tried to think of more things to be thankful for.

And she had this weekend job she loved in the re-created historic village at Seneca Valley Park. And she'd be able to finish the season out, which was good. No need for lies or awkward explanations. She'd work until winter break with nobody suspecting anything, and by the time spring came around, she'd be dead. *Did you hear,* she could imagine the regulars saying—Norm and Barb and Mary and a couple of the others—*that little high school girl who worked over the summer and on weekends died.*

Just so long as she didn't have to be the one to tell them. She sincerely hoped she would be dead by spring, rather than lingering in a state not quite dead or alive.

So, what she *didn't* have was a reason to be feeling sorry for herself. Well, no more than usual. What she *didn't* have was a reason to be crying.

But here she was, sitting at one of the round tables at the Ballston Spa Tavern, hoping that she could stop crying before the first busload of tourists came up the gravel path. *Just stop it,* she told herself, using the corner of her reproduction colonial serving-girl shawl to wipe her eyes. She was faced away from the door, and the fire Norm had started in the hearth wasn't really going yet, so her chest and face were warm, and her back and arms goose bumpy with the cold of an October morning in upstate New York. Any minute now people would arrive—day-camp kids with construction-paper name tags pinned to their jackets, Japanese businessmen bearing cameras, families who preferred the cold of off-season to the summer crowds—expecting the warm cider, which was all this particular tavern served.

The wood floor creaked behind her, and she felt a cold draft on the back of her neck, though the fire in the grate didn't gutter and she hadn't heard the front door give its characteristic squeal.

Hurriedly Emily wiped the back of her hand across her cheeks, as though brushing wisps of hair that had gotten loose from the bun under her colonial cap. She pretended to wipe at a smudge on the table with her apron. If Mr. Drake found out that customers were coming in before she was prepared, she would be in for another of his verisimilitude lectures.

"There," she said, stepping back from the table as though examining it. "That's better." She rubbed her arms. "Ooo, a bit brisk today, isn't it?" Finally she turned to see who had entered.

Not a sightseer after all. He was in colonial costume; that was the first thing she noticed—his oversized, drop-shouldered shirt that put him in the same 1750 to 1790 era she was supposed to represent, though she had never seen him before. Maybe he was subbing for someone. He even had his hair long enough to be bound at the nape of his neck, which the board of trustees didn't insist on, knowing that most of the men were part-timers whose regular employers might disapprove of a pigtail. Emily decided this guy probably wasn't employed. He couldn't have been more than a year or two older than Emily, so he was probably a student, maybe high school, maybe college. Most of the students left after the summer.

The second thing she noticed was that he was exceptionally good-looking, in a clear-skinned, innocent-eyed manner. Noticing that made her feel uncomfortable. Things being as they were, how this guy looked was none of her business.

"Yes?" she said, because the young man had said nothing. And she turned her back to him because her eyes were beginning to overflow again.

"Are you..." His voice was strained, as though he wasn't used to it. "Is there anything..."

Oh, damn, he'd realized she'd been crying. "Isn't there something you're supposed to be doing?" she asked, embarrassment putting a snap into her tone. Good; nothing wrong with that. Frighten him off.

"I'm sorry," he said. There was pain in that apology, and Emily knew she had put it there. He'd probably fought with himself, with his inclination not to get involved, and she'd gone and bitten his head off. There's maintaining your privacy, she told herself, and then there's being just plain mean. "Look." She turned back to him. "I'm the one who should—"

He'd taken a step away. "I'm sorry," he repeated, almost a whisper.

She'd put him in a panic; she could see it in those wide eyes. That gave her a wretched feeling, and she started, "Don't—"

He shook his head. "I'm sorry." He stepped back.

And dissolved into the air.

By closing time Emily had talked herself into and out of a variety of rationalizations several times over. But each of those rationalizations assumed one of two things, and since Emily refused to believe she was hallucinating—brain tumor or not—she had to assume she had seen some sort of ghost.

She put out the DISPLAY CLOSED sign, and latched the door and windows from the inside against any stragglers, then she banked down the fire. She wiped down the tables, washed the last batch of mugs, checked the supply of cider, and filled out the daily-attendance-estimate forms. The same as she did every day she worked here. Norm would be by later, as he was every day, to check that all the candles and cooking fires were truly out.

She could hear the other demonstrators and tour guides calling good night to one another outside, and the crunch of gravel carried in the crisp air as they walked down the path to the covered toll bridge that marked the entrance of the main exhibit area. To the west were several hundred acres of dense wooded area—owned by the museum and slated for development as more historic buildings were moved here from sites all along the eastern seaboard. Emily knew from experience that the trees' shadows would be long and gloomy already, reaching the Shaker meetinghouse across the commons from the tavern. Everything as it should be. Everything as it had always been, until today.

Inside the tavern, she was more aware of the smoky smell now than she'd been when the fire had actually been burning. Already her breath was visible in the chill late-afternoon air. All that was left was to douse the candles and go meet her mother in the parking lot. Then it was another evening of just her and her parents pretending everything was fine. Same as all other days.

And yet... And yet... The doubts and questions she had managed to block during her busyness of providing mulled cider and historical information and period atmosphere now rushed to fill the void inactivity created.

"Hello," she called, very softly, embarrassed even though there was no one to witness her making a fool of herself. "Are you still here? I'm..."

This was ridiculous. If Mary, who demonstrated spinning and weaving in the log cabin, happened to stop by on her way out as she sometimes did, and found Emily at this...

Mary would tell her ghosts were silly.

But what was a handsome young man with distress in his eyes, who dressed in colonial garb and dissolved in thin air?

"I'm sorry I snapped at you," she told the air. "You startled me; that's all. Please come back."

Now, what had she gone and said that for?

"Hello? Whoever you are? Are you still here?"

Facing the door she felt the draft from behind her, from within the room. "I—"

Despite herself she gasped at the sound of his voice. She whirled to face him.

"Don't...," he pleaded. Already he was beginning to shimmer at the edges, the flames from the candles on the mantel behind him faintly visible through his torso. "I'm sorry," he assured her. "I meant no harm."

"Wait!" she cried. "Don't go!"

He didn't become any more solid, but at least he didn't disappear.

"You startled me," she repeated. My God, she was talking to someone she could see right through. She backed into the table. She hadn't truly expected him to return. Now what? His face was pale between his dark hair and darker eyes. That...may have been his normal coloring. But he looked...

He looked, she realized, at least as scared of her as she was of him.

She wasn't used to having people scared of her.

"I'm sorry," she said again. "Please forgive me." The old-fashioned clothes they both wore encouraged a more formal speech.

The boy seemed to gulp.

(Could ghosts gulp?) She forced a smile. "Who are you?"

He looked desperate for something to be doing with his hands. "John." He cleared his throat. "John Mellender."

Instinctively she extended her hand as she said, "My name's Emily Nash."

He hesitated, wiped his hand on his breeches, then reached out also.

Their hands missed.

Or, rather, they didn't.

Her hand seemed to pass through cold thick air. She shuddered.

As did he. He stepped back, hugging himself as if for warmth. "What are you?" he asked.

"*What am I?*" she echoed, incredulous, thinking, *Oh, no. Don't tell me he doesn't even know he's a ghost.*

But he didn't look like a ghost, not anymore. He had fully materialized, or solidified, or whatever it was that ghosts do when you can't see the wallpaper behind them anymore. His white linen shirt had no bloodstains; nor, except for appearing paler than she'd expect for a man dressed like an eighteenth-century farmer, did he bear any obvious signs of violence or disease. Not like horror-show ghouls. What had killed him? After stepping away from her, he had put out a hand to steady himself, a hand which now solidly gripped the back of one of the tavern chairs. He looked, Emily had to admit to herself, like a man who had just seen a ghost.

"I work here," she told him. She sat down on the nearest chair, to prove to him that she was as substantial as he was. "How did you get here?"

The boy—John—thought about that for a moment.

"I don't know," he said vaguely, glancing around the room as though it wasn't at all familiar. Then he looked straight at her and repeated, "I don't know. What is this place?"

Haunting—and he didn't even know where? "The Ballston Spa Tavern."

"Ballston Spa..." He pulled around the chair he'd been holding and straddled it, facing her, close enough to...to touch. He folded his arms over the back of the chair. "I'm from Watervliet," he said. "Well, not exactly the town. My family has a farm. How did I get to be in Ballston Spa?"

She shook her head hopelessly. He looked so confused, so vulnerable. "Ballston Spa's not that far from Watervliet," she offered. She didn't have the heart to tell him that the tavern was no longer in Ballston Spa but had been transported by truck and relocated halfway across the state.

"A day away," he said, and it still would be, if you traveled by horse today. Then, more to himself, "How did I lose a whole day?"

Distressed, Emily put her hand to her mouth, then saw that John was watching her every move. She folded her hands on the table in front of her.

Never taking his eyes away from hers, John reached across the table.

She saw that his hands were clean, even under the nails. The fingers were long and slender, though the

146

palms were somewhat calloused. She could see all those details. And then again she felt the cold, the almost tangible...something...as his hand passed through hers.

John wrapped his arms around the chair back. "I think," he said, without looking directly at her, "that I may have died."

And what could she answer to that?

Maybe this was nature's way of telling her to stop feeling sorry for herself. At least she wasn't dead yet. At least she wasn't dead and just finding out about it.

"What day is today?" he asked.

"October twenty-four," she answered, and he closed his eyes. She hesitated, then finished: "In the year two thousand."

His lips moved slightly, as though he might have whispered a prayer or an oath. Or maybe he was doing the math. Not that it would have required math to see that he was at least two centuries away from home. Then he looked at her again, swallowed hard, and said, "Well. I guess the chances were always pretty good that I'd die before two thousand."

Don't, she mentally begged him. *Don't be like that.* "What..." She had to clear her throat and start again. "What is the last date you...remember?"

"April." Again he was the one who looked away. "April thirtieth, seventeen seventy-five."

That was after the battles of Lexington and Concord.

147

Too bad that by the time she had started working here, she wasn't taking American history anymore. She finally had all the dates and details down cold. Had there been fighting that early at Watervliet? He was probably a soldier, killed in the first days of the American Revolution. Should she tell him? She swallowed hard and asked, "And the last thing you remember, were you in Watervliet? At the farm?"

"Yes. No." He appeared to have suddenly noticed that his breath left no trail of vapor in the chill air as did hers. He held his palm a few inches from his mouth and breathed into it. Seeing her watching him, he got up abruptly, scraping the chair across the slats of the wooden floor. "I don't remember." Absently he rubbed the base of his collarbone, showing above the open neck of his shirt. "It almost seems—"

The tavern door rattled, then someone banged on it. "Yo!" Norm's voice called. "Emily. Still in there?"

Emily had instinctively turned at the noise, but when she looked back, she was alone in the room. It had gotten quite dark, with only the candles on the mantel, though so gradually that she hadn't noticed. She should confide in Norm, she thought, who was her parents' age but more sensible. Instead she said, "In a minute, Norm." She whispered, "John?" and peered into the corners, though she knew that wasn't where he had gone. *How sad*, she thought. *How very, very sad.*

"Emily," Norm called, "no overtime for winter hours."

Which was a joke because—like most of them—she was a volunteer and didn't get paid at all.

"Right," she said. She pulled her shawl tight around her shoulders as she fumbled with the door latch, her fingers clumsy with the cold. She hadn't noticed that, either.

At home Emily started to tell her parents about what had happened—several times she started, then couldn't find the right words. Finally she blurted it out as they sat watching some inane game show on TV. The TV was always on lately. Nobody liked the silence anymore. In the middle of the game's final round, Emily said, "I met a ghost today."

She saw her mother stiffen, but her father went for playing it light. "Oh, yes?" he asked. "Worked the Octagon House?" The Octagon House was the only building in the museum reported to be haunted—and those reports were seriously frowned upon by the management. Still, those who worked there insisted that tools would disappear only to be located elsewhere the following day. Emily had always found it hard to understand why someone would cross the boundary between life and death just to borrow a carpenter's plumb or to play hide-and-seek with Eunice Goungo's reading glasses.

"I was at the tavern," she told him. She'd been assigned there regularly since summer.

"Ah! More and more interesting. Some bold pirate, come to dig up his treasure from under the barroom floor?" He ran his fingers up and down her arm to simulate goose bumps.

She didn't like being tickled. Hadn't since she'd been about five. Surely after all these years he must have noticed. But in many ways both her parents seemed to be trying to go back to the more carefree time of her early childhood, presenting her with gifts of stuffed animals and talking to her as though she were barely able to reason. She folded her arms across her chest. "Pirates in Ballston Spa?" she asked.

"Hmm. Maybe a more recent ghost. Got it. That old lady who choked on the cider last month. She only seemed to recover but went home and died." Emily's mother looked ready to strangle him, but he was apparently oblivious. He finished, "And now she's come back to haunt you because it's all your fault."

"Not funny," her mother said from between clenched teeth. Did she think she was a ventriloquist, Emily wondered, and that they wouldn't be able to guess who had spoken even though there were only the three of them in the room?

"It wasn't a little old lady," Emily said. "It was a young man from seventeen seventy-five."

"Can't be that young," her father reasoned. "If he's

from seventeen seventy-five, he's got to be at least two hundred and twenty-five years old."

"He only looked about seventeen or eighteen," Emily said.

Her mother got up and walked out of the room.

"What?" her father called after his wife.

"Unresolved issues," Emily said. *Unresolved issues* was one of the support group's favorite terms. She got up, too, but headed in the opposite direction.

"What'd I say?" her father called after her.

On TV the people from the show were waving to the camera as the closing music played.

"I never know what to say anymore," her father complained to the screen.

Winter hours—what the staff at Seneca Valley Museum called winter hours—were actually fall and spring hours: 9:30 to 4:30, Saturdays and Sundays only. There were no real winter hours because after the Harvest Festival on the last weekend in October, the museum locked its doors until mid-April.

Emily had met her ghost the second to the last Sunday in October.

What difference does that make? she asked herself. But it did make a difference.

Monday morning, after her parents had left for work

and before her school bus came, she tried calling out to John Mellender, but he didn't come. He must somehow be linked with the tavern, she reasoned—even if he hadn't recognized that tavern or known why he was there. She had hoped that someone who could travel freely through time would have no difficulty with the five-mile journey between the museum and her home. *How awful,* she thought, *to be so young and dead.* But she'd met kids who were younger who were going to be dead soon. *She* was going to be dead soon. How awful, she amended her thought, to be so young and lost and frightened and alone. To be dead and not even know how.

But there was more to it than that.

She didn't talk to anybody at school about what had happened at the museum. She hadn't told any of them about her illness, and she no longer talked to them about anything important—if she ever had. And if she'd ever been close to any of them before, she couldn't remember it. They were background noise, like the TV. They didn't avoid her; they included her in their conversations, but more and more she found herself losing track of what they were saying. The first many times that this happened, somebody would laughingly catch her up on what she'd missed. But then the laughter stopped. And lately they just talked around her. So, these were not the people to confide in, to tell about seeing a ghost.

After school, despite telling herself several times that

she was being foolish, she rode her bicycle to the museum. It was locked, of course, as she had known it would be. But she stood in the deserted parking lot and called John Mellender's name. She waited, her hands jammed into the pockets of her sweater as the wind pushed against her back, whipping her hair—the hair she was fortunate she hadn't lost to chemo—about her face. Bright orange pamphlets from the museum flapped against the fence, along with leaves, which had lost all their gay colors and were now just brown and brittle debris. Dead. Dead leaves.

When she got cold enough, she got on her bike and pedaled the long way home.

Saturday morning Emily hoped to get to the museum village early, to give herself extra time before she had to open the tavern. But her mother wanted to talk.

"Is everything all right, Em?" "Em" was her nickname back from when she'd called herself that as a baby, too little to get her mouth around the syllables of Emily. She'd been asking her parents since fourth grade to call her Emily, and they'd been pretty good about it until recently, when they reverted.

"Yeah," Emily said. "Fine."

"You just seem so...quiet...lately. Your father and I are worried."

"I'm fine," Emily repeated.

"You seem to be taking more of your pain medication."

Emily shrugged. It was just a headache. But—because of where the tumor was—her mother wouldn't believe it was just a headache.

Her mother said, "Because any time you want to talk..."

Emily let the unfinished sentence hang there. What could talking solve?

"*Do* you want to talk?" her mother asked.

"I want to get to work on time," Emily said.

Then, because her mother looked crushed by the rejection, Emily added, "It's good therapy for me."

Her mother brightened at that. Support group was all for not feeling sorry for yourself. "Just don't work too hard," she said. "Don't let yourself get worn-out."

In the end, by the time her mother dropped her off in front of the administration building, she was even slightly later than usual. Emily fairly flew down the path, past the Old-Fashioned Sweet Shoppe, around the gazebo, through the covered toll bridge, past the blacksmith shop and the apothecary, to the Ballston Spa Tavern. She slammed the door behind her and called, "John, are you there?"

The air shimmered, and she was so relieved she forgot herself: She went to hug him.

John stepped back, and only her arm passed coldly through his arm. "What's happened?" he asked. "What's wrong?"

Her arm was numb to the elbow with the cold, and she stood rubbing it, having been brought up short. "I... was just happy to see you."

His aloofness dissolved into a smile. "I'm happy to see you too, Emily."

She said, "I kept thinking about you all week, worrying about you."

The smile faltered. "All...week?"

"Since the last time you were here."

"It's been a week?"

Emily nodded. She could see him accept what she said without understanding why it should be so. "John," she asked, and her voice quivered, "where are you when you're not here?"

He considered, then shook his head.

"Why did you come here?"

"You called me," he told her.

"The first time."

Again he paused to consider. He repeated, more slowly, "You called me." He sat in one of the chairs and rested his elbows on the table. "I...heard you crying..."

"While you were at your farm?" she prompted.

"Yes. No. I don't know where I was. I heard you crying and..." He looked at her quizzically. "I knew... somehow...that you were thinking of taking your life."

That was a cold draft up Emily's back, colder even than seeing John disappear that first time. It had been a thought. On and off, when the world closed in on her, when she tired of fighting a battle she knew she could never win—it had been a thought. Rarely verbalized, certainly never acted upon, always there as an option: Wouldn't it be easier now rather than later?

He must have been able to tell from her face that he hadn't been wrong. "And," he continued, "I thought: She can't do that. She doesn't..." He blinked, then finished in a very small voice. "She doesn't know what it's like to be dead."

Emily sat down at the same table. Heavily. *Not yet,* she could have said. *I don't know yet.* Instead, she asked, "You remember now? Being dead? Dying?"

"No." He rubbed his arms as though cold. "Don't die, Emily," he said.

"Everybody dies eventually," she said. She ached with the realization that she couldn't take his hand. He could touch his own chest, the furniture, everything but her. "It's just..." She couldn't say it. She was starting to cry again, and she sniffled, angry with herself. "It's just so pointless."

John reached to wipe the tears, and the touch felt like an ice cube on her cheek. He snatched his hand back in obvious frustration.

Someone tapped at the still-closed shutter. "*Ssst,* Emily," Mary hissed. "Drake's coming. Better get a move on."

John stood, with that scared look, but didn't disappear.

Emily got rid of her own tears. "Yes. Almost ready," she lied. How could she have forgotten the Harvest Festival? Hayrides in the meadow, minuteman maneuvers on the green, apple bobbing in the town square. All sorts of extra programs. Lots of visitors before the closedown for the season. Mr. Drake would be semihysterical all weekend and breathing down everybody's neck.

They could hear Mary's footsteps hurrying down the path as she continued on her way.

"Right," John said to Emily. "What needs doing?"

"Mugs out," Emily said, "cider poured, shutters opened...Oh, damn!" She'd nearly tripped over a box that one of the workers had brought in some time before she arrived.

John had already gone behind the bar and was getting the mugs. "What?"

"Snickerdoodles."

He gave her a blank look.

"They're these colonial cookies—"

"I know what they are," he said, sounding exasperated.

"I'm supposed to make some." She started pulling supplies out of the box: ingredients, bowls, cooking utensils. The cider was provided year-round; the snickerdoodles only for special occasions, like Harvest Festival Weekend.

"This is an *inn*," John objected.

"Yes, but we don't have a license from New York State to serve alcohol, so we serve cider and snickerdoodles instead."

"'New York *State*'?" he repeated in amazement.

She shook her head, indicating there was no time to explain, and started measuring out the sugar.

John opened the shutters, started the cider heating, and tossed a handful of cinnamon onto the fire, which made the tavern smell as though she'd been baking for an hour. She smiled at him, and he blew her a kiss.

A moment later, as the first tourist started to push open the door, he was gone.

"Why are the people who come here dressed so oddly?" John asked.

Emily, who was just closing the door behind the day's last sightseers, jumped.

"I'm sorry," he said, seeing her startle. He went to put his hand on her shoulder, then yanked it away as cold seeped between them. "I'm sorry," he said again. Getting that panicked look in his eyes. Again.

"It's all right," she assured him, though she imagined this was what advanced frostbite felt like, and she had to work to keep the pain off her face. Doubly so now. Her head had been throbbing all afternoon from the stress of cooking, and answering the same questions over and over, and remembering to smile. "John. It's all right." She had to fight her own inclination to offer a comforting hand. "John, I want to try something." She opened the tavern door. "Can you leave this building?"

"I don't know." He went out onto the stoop. Then, looking back at her, he stepped onto the gravel.

Almost giddy with relief, Emily followed; and they started down the walkway, which circled the commons, away from the dark woods whose shadows grew longer daily with the approach of winter.

John shook his head in amazement. "It's so changed. These buildings weren't here."

That was encouraging. "I thought you couldn't remember the Ballston Spa Tavern."

"I"—he realized what he was saying—"can't." He got that faraway look he sometimes did, as though he was listening to internal voices, or was on the verge of remembering something. "No," he said, slowly. "I *do*. Samuel..."

"Who?"

Finally he met her eyes again. "My brother, Samuel, and I. We came to Ballston Spa to deliver a horse my father had sold to a man named Darius Bartlett. Why couldn't I remember that before?"

"I don't know," Emily said. "Did you deliver the horse?"

He thought about it. "Yes."

"And then what?"

Again the hesitation. But this time John shook his head. "Did you meet Bartlett at the tavern?"

Just when she was about to give up, he said, "No. At his house."

Robbery? she wondered. Had Bartlett killed him for the horse? She asked, "Did he—"

"We left the house," John interrupted her, but he was speaking slowly again, as though having trouble reconstructing what had happened.

"And came...," she prompted, "to the tavern?"

He bit his lip and shook his head. "I don't remember."

"It seems as though whatever happened must have—"

"I don't remember." He had stopped and now closed his eyes as though in pain.

"What is it? John?"

He had taken a step back. His hand closed convulsively at the opening of his shirt, over where his heart would be. If ghosts had hearts.

"John?" She was getting scared now. "It's all right," she said. "It's not important. You don't have to remember."

"I can't go any farther," he whispered.

She saw that they were almost at the covered bridge, which led out of the exhibition area of the museum, away from the old buildings, toward the modern. "All right," she told him. "We'll go back."

"I can't"—he took another step back—"go any..."— and another.

"John—"

He dissolved.

"—don't go," she finished in a whisper. She realized that her headache must have gone, because now it was suddenly back.

Mary, coming up the path from the log house, said, "Zoo day, huh? See you tomorrow."

Emily watched as Mary walked through the bridge and cut across the green toward the gift shop. She hadn't seen him.

She hadn't seen him.

Silently Emily followed, and it wasn't until halfway through dinner that she remembered she hadn't banked the fire in the tavern, or cleaned up at all.

After thinking that she would never fall asleep, Emily was dreaming about John Mellender. On one level she knew she was asleep. She replayed moments with him over and over, recapturing looks, nuances: the slight catch in his voice when he stepped away from her that first time, apologizing for frightening her; the shy smile; the way he always seemed to be hugging himself for warmth; glancing up, for the briefest moment, before saying, "I think that I may have died." She lingered, consciously, unable to let it rest.

But on another level it seemed so real—so very real. So that when she started to fantasize, when she started to embroider what had happened and take it a step further, she could feel her heart quicken, her breath catch. She imagined his warm breath as he came close, closer than he had ever really come. His lips touched hers, gently, lovingly. He caressed her hair, her shoulders. He told her she was beautiful, which she knew she was not. He told her he loved her, which...Oh, God. She replayed the smile, the fleeting glance. Which maybe...

Maybe.

His breath quickened to match hers. She felt his heart beating as he held her, kissed her neck. She flung her arms around him and clung to him.

And then she awakened.

Her father, or her mother, snored softly in the next room. The hall clock ticked. A car passed outside.

Emily held herself very still, forcing herself not to make a sound. *How stupid*, she thought. She was *dying*. What was she doing falling in love? *Obviously* this relationship had no future.

And he was already dead.

That in itself, she told herself as she got up to get some medicine for her headache, probably pretty much ruled out a traditional church wedding.

Sunday morning.

The last day the museum would be open until spring.

Her last chance to see John Mellender.

At breakfast her father said, "Your mother and I think you should stay home today."

Her mother had the sense not to be in the room at the time.

"Why?" Emily demanded.

"We think maybe you're working a bit too hard, getting a bit overtired."

"No," Emily said.

"All the same." Her father sipped his coffee as though that had settled that.

"I want to go to work," Emily said. "It's all I have."

"Nonsense," her father said. "You have us. You have your school friends. Take the day off. Relax."

"I *need* to go to work today."

Her father frowned. She knew he hated confrontation. He said, "Surely they can get along without you."

"Of course they can get along without me," she said, mentally adding, *They'll have to get along without me in the spring.* But she didn't say anything about leaving them short-staffed. Instead she said, "This is something I need to do for myself. To give myself a sense of completeness, of closure." Support group was always good for psychobabble.

"It's just, you get so caught up in it," her father said, but he was weakening, she could tell. "Your mother says that yesterday you came out to the parking lot without your jacket."

"I was talking to somebody and I forgot," she explained. "I wasn't cold until Mom started telling me how cold it was. Please drive me there."

She saw her father glance upward—asking for divine advice or gauging if Emily's mother was about to come downstairs and demand to know why her orders were being questioned. He sighed, and she knew she had won one more day with John.

Somebody had taken care of both the hearth and the cleaning, Emily noted guiltily. Had to have been Norm. Poor overworked, underappreciated Norm. Well, she appreciated him, but the board of trustees didn't. She hid her winter coat behind the bar, with the jacket she had left there yesterday.

"John," she called.

"Emily." He appeared out of nowhere.

"Are you all right?" she asked, which had to be the world's dumbest question. He was, after all, two hundred years dead. "What happened yesterday?" she asked.

He shook his head, rubbing his arms as though for warmth. It was freezing in here today. Norm hadn't been in yet, and this morning there had been a sprinkling of frost on the ground of the common. Emily gritted her teeth to keep them from chattering.

John leaned against the bar. He had gone from rubbing his arms to resting his hand at his open-necked shirt—to the place where a live man's heart would be. He saw her watching and seemed to suddenly become aware of what he was doing. He lowered his hand. Slowly.

Even clenching her teeth couldn't get them to stop chattering now.

He met her eyes. "I remember how I died."

Did she want to hear this?

"How?" she asked, so softly he might not have even heard but only guessed from the movement of her lips.

He looked down at his hand again. "I was shot." He closed his eyes and shivered. In a moment he'd regained control and shrugged as though apologizing for his weakness. His hand twitched once as he let it drop to his side.

Emily licked her lips. "I'm sorry. I'm so sorry." She wanted so much to take him into her arms. Her eyes filled with tears.

"Don't cry," he said. "It was a long time ago." He forced a smile. "Even if I'm only just now finding out about it."

"Stupid war," she said. She'd never before thought of the American Revolution as being stupid, but that's just what it was.

John's eyes grew wide. "There was a war?"

"I thought..." But then she remembered what a loose confederation the colonies had been in 1775, and how slowly news would travel, especially to the smaller towns and villages.

John gave a low whistle. Unconsciously his hand went back to his chest as he paced the room. He glanced up sharply. "With the King?" he asked. "That's what you mean: a war of independence?"

She nodded.

"There was talk...I never thought...Who won?"

"Uh, we did. The colonies."

He nodded, biting his lip. "I don't think this had anything to do with that," he said.

"You weren't a soldier?"

"Lord, no!"

"Not involved with politics?"

He shook his head.

"What about this man Bartlett you mentioned yesterday?"

"I don't think he was the one."

She waited for him to say something else.

"I remember...Samuel and I came here after delivering the horse." He paused, looking at the door. "I... opened the door..." He shuddered. Turned away. "There was a man. Sitting..."—he indicated a specific spot— "here. I remember a gun..." He was clutching his heart; his breathing was loud and ragged. "The door opened. I...The door opened—"

Someone kicked in the door.

Emily took in a breath halfway between gasp and scream.

"Sorry," Norm said. He was lugging in her supplies for the day's snickerdoodles and cider. "Didn't mean to scare you."

Now Emily had *her* hand to *her* heart. There was no sign of John. "Sorry about yesterday," she managed to say. "I forgot."

"That's okay," Norm said, too polite to ask how anybody could possibly forget something like putting out the fire. "Except..."

"What?" Emily pulled her shawl tighter, but that didn't stop the shivering. "Norm?"

"Drake was making the rounds with me."

Emily winced. "Mad?"

From Norm's expression, *mad* didn't begin to cover it. "He wants you to work the log cabin today with Barb. Mary'll be here."

"The log cabin!" Emily cried. She hated that. Spinning, she kept getting flax up her nose, and she wasn't good enough at weaving to keep from smacking the back of her hand on the loom. Besides, it was a two-person demonstration and she wouldn't have a minute to herself. "Norm!"

"Sorry." Not that it was his fault. "Drake said..."

"Drake said *what*?" she demanded when Norm hesitated.

Norm had obviously reconsidered, and he shrugged. "Well, you know Drake. Nothing important."

"Drake said what?"

Norm shrugged again and wouldn't meet her eyes. "Mary's more reliable. And Barb'll keep you on your toes at the log cabin. Sorry."

Emily stomped out of the tavern, never pausing for her jacket or coat.

Mary, just coming up the path, smiled apologetically, then said, "My gosh, Emily! Don't you have a coat? It's supposed to snow today."

Emily ignored her, though it was hardly Mary's fault. Damn Drake. Today was the last day. Damn it. For once she wanted to scream out her news: *I'm dying, dammit! Humor me!*

The morning dragged forever. She planned to go someplace where she could be alone during her lunch break—one of the unattended displays—to talk to John one last time. And that was all that kept her going. She wouldn't let herself consider the possibility that he might be able to come to her only in the tavern.

Her loom thumped noisily, counterpoint to the whirring of Barb's spinning wheel. If she could have ripped her throbbing head off her body, she would have. Her hands shook as she poured three pills into her hand—only one more than she was supposed to take—

and swallowed them without water. When she couldn't get that damn childproof cap back on, she flung it across the room. Barb watched her anxiously, but Emily pretended not to notice. Neither spoke, except to the tourists.

Four hours till lunch.

Three and a half hours.

Three hours and twenty minutes.

Three hours.

Drake came in at two hours and forty-five minutes while she was trying to demonstrate, for a family who didn't speak English, how to card wool. He gave her one of his baleful looks, but he wasn't going to say anything in front of the visitors. After about two minutes of that, Emily threw the shuttle across the room, called Drake a flatulent asshole, and strode out of the log cabin.

She left him to explain *that* to the family and went to the Shaker meetinghouse, the closest building that didn't have a regular attendant.

"John!" she called. She was shaking, afraid he couldn't hear her call, except in the tavern.

But, "Yes," he said. He was sitting on the back of one of the benches in the men's half of the room, his feet up on the pew behind.

She started to run up the aisle to him, then remembered at the last moment. She stopped, helpless, and sank to her knees and began to cry.

"Emily." He scrambled down and rushed to her, and caught himself just in time, a hand upraised just short of brushing the tear-dampened hair from her face.

"This is the last day," she said between sobs. "The museum closes in another few hours, and it won't open again until spring, and I won't be able to come here, and you won't be able to come out." Miserable, she finished, "I'll never last through the winter."

He crouched before her. "Oh, Emily," he sighed. "You will."

She realized he thought she was speaking figuratively. "I'm dying," she said. Did they know about cancer in the 1700s? They might well have called it something else. "I have a disease of the brain. That's probably"—she wasn't even sure how she meant this—"why I can see you."

He reached for her, unable to hold her but sending icicles through her shoulder where his hand passed through. "Emily," he said. "I'm so sorry."

"I need to know," she said, because otherwise—ha!—the curiosity would kill her. No, it was more than curiosity; it was wanting the world to be an orderly place. She asked, "Who shot you?"

John sighed. "A jealous husband."

Well, that was orderly, even if not quite the order she had envisioned. Everything fell into place. The world made sense after all. It was her turn to say, "Oh, John, I'm sorry."

He had his arms wrapped tight around himself. "You don't understand," he said. "I was mistaken for someone else. I was killed by mistake."

Very slowly, very carefully, Emily put her arms around him. It was like being in a lake, like trying to hold on to a cold current. For a few seconds, they managed it. Then her hand slipped through his neck, and his through her back, and they were left sitting on their heels, both of them shivering.

Behind her the door to the meetinghouse flew open. She expected John to disappear the way he had other times, but he didn't.

Behind her, her father's voice said, "Jeez, Em."

"See why I called you?" she heard Drake say. "She's been like this all weekend—talking to herself, leaving fires unattended, popping pills."

"Don't you see him?" Emily asked them, looking directly at John.

"Emily, it's all right," her father said. He took her by the shoulders and turned her around. "It's probably just the medicine. We'll get your medications balanced properly—"

She craned around and saw that John was gone. "John!" she called. "Come back!"

Her father was struggling out of his coat, and he got it around her shoulders. "It's her medication," he explained to Drake. "She's under a doctor's care, but there must be something wrong with the mix she's taking..." He was trying to rub warmth into her hands. "Here"—he got her to her feet—"all right now?"

"Yes," she said. Then she pushed her father into Drake, and she fled, her father's coat falling to the floor behind her.

"Emily!" she heard her father yell.

She ran across the commons, past the Ballston Spa Tavern, into the woods behind—the woods slated for great things by the board of trustees, things she knew she would never see.

The trees in the woods were thick enough to hide her, even with most of their leaves already on the ground. Emily fought through the underbrush, slid down a slope of rocks and tree stumps, followed a frozen stream ever deeper into the woods.

I'll cross the stream, she thought, but of course the ice was just a thin crust in October, and she went right through, so that she slipped and landed sitting in the icy water. She picked herself up and fled farther into the woods until she lost all sense of time and direction. Her wet skirt stiffened frostily, chafing against her legs.

"Emily!" she heard off and on. Her father. Norm. Strangers on bullhorns. But they were faint, distant.

Still, she kept on running, to put more distance between them. Her plan was to wait until night, then return to the tavern, hoping they'd give up before she would.

Once she got warm, once she rested, she'd be able to think what to do next. She tripped and fell to her knees and stayed there, her teeth chattering. She'd get up as soon as she got enough energy.

But she was too tired, and she put her head down on a pile of dry leaves. She hadn't smelled leaves—really smelled them—since she'd been seven or eight. She'd forgotten how wonderful they smelled. She closed her eyes, just for a minute, just to get her strength back.

"Emily," she heard, a gentle but insistent whisper near her ear, and she groaned. "Emily, you have to go back before it's too late."

"It's too late already," she whispered back. "I can't move. I've frozen to the ground."

Hands grasped her shoulders, strong, solid hands that forced her to sit up, that held her close, rocking her until finally, finally, she was warm again.

They didn't find her body till spring.

Being Dead

New York, October 1930

Until the part where I died, my day had been going pretty well.

I'd sold all but one of my papers, I'd earned seventy-five cents in tips, and all I needed was to sell that last paper and I could go home. Then along came this swell—in suit and hat, with a briefcase—and he handed me a dollar bill.

At least that's what I thought it was at first. I was digging into my pocket to get him the change when I took a closer look and saw it was a twenty. I was going to ask him if he was crazy—like I'd have enough money to make change for a twenty—but when I looked up, he was already halfway down the block.

"Mister!" I called after him. "Hey, mister!"

He never even slowed down. I had to run after him, and when I caught up and told him he'd given me a twenty and I didn't have near enough to give him his change, he looked at me like I was talking Chinese.

"It's all gone," he told me in this hollow distracted voice. "All of it."

"Yeah," I said. Banks and businesses had been failing since the stock market had crashed back in October last year. The technical term was *depression*. But even as I tried to hand this guy back his twenty, he started walking again. Me, if I learned that I'd just lost all my money, the last thing I'd do with what I had left was tip a newsboy nineteen dollars and ninety-three cents for the newspaper that told me about it.

But I wasn't going to knock him down and *force* him to take his money. "Are you sure?" I yelled after him, because my mother would fret when she saw how much extra I had, demanding of me: "You're not turning into a crook, are you?" My mother had a fierce worry of her kids turning into crooks, seeing as we didn't have a father to keep us straight. But the guy kept walking, and even my mother would have to admit I'd tried.

So I was headed home—with an extra twenty dollars beyond my seventy-five cents in tips and what I'd have to pay DeMarco for the next edition. I was feeling real pleased with myself but not so cocky that I wasn't keeping an eye out. Some of the bigger boys think that jumping a newsboy is easy pickings. And I was also keeping a look-out on the street because in New York people always drive like crazy, and that's not even counting that yesterday's paper told about some guy who'd lost everything and figured life wasn't worth living anymore and had run his fancy car into a light pole.

So there I was, looking left and right on the sidewalk for toughs, and on the street for crazy drivers, checking out what was in front of me, and being alert to what was going on behind. The one direction I didn't think to look was up.

I heard a long drawn-out yell, and I had time to look up and see a guy above me, who seemed to be trying to claw his way back up the air to whatever window or roof top he was falling from. Which left him aimed rear-end-first at me.

And it was a big rear end.

I pick myself up off the sidewalk. There isn't any "Oh! I wonder what happened," or "Who could that possibly be lying on the sidewalk looking so much like me?"

My momma didn't raise no dummies.

I know right away that I'm dead.

There's a guy that looks to be about two hundred and fifty pounds lying on top of me, and he's dead, too. Even though I can see him lying there motionless on the sidewalk, at the same time I can see him sitting up, shaking his head as though to clear it. "Is it too late to change my mind?" he asks. His sitting-up self's mouth moves. His

other self continues to lie there. He looks like a double exposure, like a picture where someone forgot to advance
the film. I must look the same, lying on the sidewalk beneath him, standing on the sidewalk several feet away,
watching.

From somewhere else—from all around us and from
inside us—a Voice says, "Welcome, Johnny. Welcome,
Stewart."

The air is sparkly, the way it is sometimes when there's
a sunny morning after the first snowfall of the year. Not
that there's snow—not in October—or sun, either, for
that matter. There usually isn't. We're talking New York
here. But the sky is as bright and blue as some kid's Cray-
ola drawing, and even though people are screaming and
pointing and beginning to gather around, none of that
bothers me, because the world is just so peaceful and
beautiful.

The Voice says, "Welcome home." It's a nice voice. It's
a voice like one of those classy radio announcers, friendly
and calming and soothing. Sort of like Lowell Thomas,
only not so full of himself.

Even though there's just the Voice, I have the impres-
sion of arms held wide to welcome me.

Stewart—I'm assuming the fat guy's name is Stewart,
since the Voice is right about me being Johnny—Stewart
has to elbow his way out from the crowd of people ringing
around where our bodies are. Though one or two of them

glance around at his passing, looking momentarily puzzled, most of them seem unaware of him.

"Me, too?" Stewart asks. "Am I allowed to come, too? Even though…I…you know…"

The Voice finishes for him, "Jumped. Yes. All who wish to come may."

This is a nice thought in theory, but I can't help but look at Stewart in a new light. "You *jumped*?" I ask.

Stewart hesitates, as though worried this might be some kind of test. "I changed my mind," he says, "halfway down."

"You landed on me," I protest.

"Sorry," Stewart says.

"'*Sorry*'?" I repeat. "You jump out a window, flatten me, *kill* me, and all you have to say for yourself is 'Sorry'?"

Stewart still looks like he thinks this is a test. "I'm very sorry?" He phrases it like a question, like he's wondering if *that* is the answer that will satisfy me.

The Voice takes Stewart's side. The Voice says, "Mistakes in judgment happen."

I cross my arms over my chest and glare at Stewart.

"I'd lost all my money," Stewart tells me.

"Yeah?" My mother and me, we keep our money in an old jar under a bunch of towels in the closet—all twelve dollars and thirty-five cents of it—so there won't be any losing that, unless somebody breaks in and steals it.

The Voice says, "All that is over now. You are coming

home, where there is no money, no pain. This is what you were created for."

And I know the Voice is right—I have a sense of a place more wonderful than Coney Island, better than talkies at the movies, more glorious than Christmas morning when someone you love is about to open the present you got for them that you know is the one thing they want most in the world.

But even with all that, I remember the extra twenty dollars in my pocket. Sure. *Now* money doesn't count. My family, which is me and my mother and my little sister, Rosie, we never had any money, even before my dad decided to go back to Ireland three years ago—from where he was supposed to send back for us, but he must of forgot. I'd always figured we weren't likely to ever get any money, and I just couldn't see that things were going to be all that different, depression or not. Then, in one moment I get as much money as my mother has been able to save in three years.

And the next moment, Stewart happens.

I find myself muttering, "It isn't fair."

"There, there," the Voice says soothingly.

"It isn't fair," I repeat.

The Voice waits. I just stand there thinking *I* didn't make any choices, *I* didn't make any mistakes—except for not looking up, of course.

"Are you saying," the Voice asks me, but not unkindly, "that you'd rather stay here and sulk?"

I think about it.

And because the Voice has spoken not unkindly, I answer, "Yes. Please."

"You may change your mind at any time," the Voice assures me. "When you're ready, you will be welcome home."

I nod to show I understand.

"How about you, Stewart?" the Voice asks.

And I see Stewart start to follow the Voice. They are taking a path that I can't actually see, but I can somehow sense. What I sense is raspberry ripple ice cream, which I know sounds strange, but anyone who's ever been dead would know exactly what I mean.

And then they are gone. And I have to decide where *I* should go.

Not home, I think. I can't bear the thought of inflicting my dead self on my family. But I'm sure I'll think of something.

Just as Stewart left without a backward glance, I turn away from the me that's lying on the sidewalk beneath Stewart's considerable bulk.

And who should I see but that scum of all scums, De-Marco. He's probably coming to check up on me. He does that all the time—sneaks up to spy on his newsboys to make sure we aren't cheating him. *Us* cheat *him*. Right. DeMarco always tries to gyp the newsboys who are new enough or dumb enough not to watch his every move. "Yeah, yeah," he's famous for saying, "I gave you three dozen papers," when he's only handed out thirty, or Sunday papers without the comics—which some people wouldn't mind, but a lot of them buy the Sunday paper just to get the comics.

Now DeMarco passes right through me, which is a sensation like standing in front of a huge fan that turns on full blast and then a second later turns off. He never even slows down. No glimmer of recognition from him that there's anything there.

"Stand back. Give us room here." DeMarco is always one for shouting orders and throwing his weight around— even though his weight isn't much: DeMarco is one of those skinny, nervous guys that's through-and-through mean.

He pushes at the crowd. Some of these people are standing around because they wish there was something they could do to help, though there clearly isn't. Some are curious, wanting to be close enough so they can be the big shots later on, saying, "I was there, I saw every-thing, this is what I know happened..." Others need to be there because they know it could have been them. These are the ones who will go home and say, "If I'd been walk-ing a little slower..." or, "If I hadn't stopped to pat the dog...," shaking with relief that it wasn't them. DeMarco shoves all these people aside, and when one of them objects, saying, "Hey—" DeMarco flashes his card that says PRESS, and no one is suspicious enough to take a closer look and see that DeMarco is a newspaper seller, not a newspaper reporter. The pass is only meant to get him into the newspaper building. But the card gives him respectability, even among the would-be big shots, and the last of them part before him.

I'm not sure what to make of all this, since I've known DeMarco for three years and I've never seen him be concerned about anything besides DeMarco. But here he is kneeling in the grit of the sidewalk where some of the more helpful of the bystanders have rolled Stewart off me. Not that I get all misty-eyed about this or anything—I figure DeMarco has to have some angle.

DeMarco grunts when he sees my body. "One of our newsboys," he says in his attempt at a sentimental voice, which I don't believe for a moment. "What a waste, what a waste."

He bows his head solemnly for a moment in what might be prayer but is more likely so no one will notice his cold, calculating eyes.

I get a nasty feeling in the pit of my stomach, excepting, of course, that I no longer have a stomach.

"Poor tyke," he says. "His mother will be devastated."

Tyke? Tyke? Like I'm some toddler still in short pants.

And then he does what I've somehow been afraid he'll do, though I'm not sneaky enough to have ever guessed it: He reaches into my body's pocket.

"That's mine!" I yell. Of course nobody can hear me. "Put that back!" I yell, anyway. I try to snatch the money away, and my hand passes straight through it. I'm close enough to see DeMarco's eyes widen in surprise, but it's not from sensing me; it's because he's seen how much I have. He *knows* I wasn't selling enough papers to be carrying this amount of money.

"Excuse me," one of the bystanders says, hesitantly, at the sight of DeMarco pawing through my pocket.

"It's quite all right," DeMarco says. "This is the money he collected for the newspaper. Let me just get this straightened out before the police and the ambulance get here. You know how *those* people are—the money'll disappear and then his poor mother will get stuck having to pay for the papers." He shakes his head to show how disgusted he is at the thought of this.

The crowd murmurs gullibly.

DeMarco gets a pair of money collection envelopes out of his pocket and puts the majority of the money in one and makes that disappear back into his pocket fast. On the other envelope, on which he scrawls my mother's name, he puts forty cents. *Forty cents! All* of the money is mine because DeMarco makes us pay for our papers up front: I've already paid for what I've sold, and I'm not likely to be needing to buy the next edition. But here he is, looking all sad and gooey over that envelope with the forty cents. And then, as though coming to a great humanitarian decision, he mumbles like he can't help how sentimental he is, "You know, the poor woman could use the extra," and he gets one dollar from his own pocket and slips that into the envelope for my mother. One dollar. In place of more than twenty. A few of the bystanders wipe tears from their eyes at this poignant generosity. I try to kick DeMarco, but my foot passes through him.

"This is not fair!" I shout.

One of the bystanders looks up, not *at* me, but kind of/sort of in my direction. And she has a quizzical, listening expression on her face.

"He's stealing my money!" I shout directly at her since she seems more inclined to hear me than the others.

She *can* hear me. I can tell by the way she glances around. But what she's glancing around at is the other people. And she can tell they have heard nothing. She's looking at DeMarco, and her eyes go to the pocket where he's put the envelope with the dollar and forty cents for my mother. But then she looks around again, sees no one else is suspicious, and she looks away.

"He's stealing money from the dead!" I shout. And my words stir her to action.

She hunches her shoulders, sticks her hands in her pockets, ducks her head down—and she walks away.

"Hey!" I yell after her. "Hey!"

She walks faster.

I take a few steps after her, but there's no point in making her life miserable. If I'm going to go after someone—let it be DeMarco.

And speaking of DeMarco, he isn't finished yet.

Now he says, "Anybody know the poor jumper?"

Heads shake and no one seems to suspect that's glee in DeMarco's expression as he says, "This is the worst part of my job—breaking this kind of news to the family." DeMarco goes ahead and reaches into Stewart's pocket. For someone who killed himself because he didn't have any money, Stewart's wallet looks pretty fat. But DeMarco makes a big show of ignoring the bills and goes straight for the identification. He gets a notebook out of his own pocket, and he writes down Stewart's name and address.

I figure he's going to palm Stewart's money before he puts the wallet back in Stewart's pocket; but before he has a chance, a cop finally comes on the scene. He walks right through me, too, like I'm the only free spot on the sidewalk.

"He stole my money!" I yell at the cop, but he's not as receptive as the lady I chased off.

"All right, all right," the cop says, "those of you who saw what happened, stick around a bit. The rest of you, keep moving. We don't need a circus here."

He crouches next to DeMarco, who says, "Jumper,"

and hands over Stewart's wallet. He's missed his chance to clean it out, but he makes sure the cop sees his PRESS card and the notebook on which he's written Stewart's name and address. He reads Stewart's name out loud, in case the cop has made it on to the police force without knowing how to read. He tells the cop my name, too, and tells him where I live. I don't even want to think about my mother getting the news.

One of the bystanders tells the cop, "Maybe you should consider counting the money out now, here in front of everybody, just to make sure the family ends up ever seeing it."

The crowd murmurs approvingly.

"Yeah?" the cop says. "Maybe you should consider not being such a wiseacre, just to make sure you don't get your head knocked."

Meanwhile, DeMarco has stood up, and he's making his way through the press of people.

"Stop, thief!" I yell. They always ask, "Where's a cop when you need one?" Here I've got the cop, and he's worthless. I stamp my foot in frustration.

And the lightbulb in the nearest street lamp explodes.

Everybody jumps in surprise, including me. I didn't do that.

Did I?

Nah, I tell myself. Coincidence. Gotta be. I think. I'm 90 percent sure. But I try stamping my foot again.

The cop fumbles Stewart's wallet, and it drops from his hand.

Whoa! This is getting spooky.

I turn my face up at the sky and yell, "Excuse me..."

"Yes," the Voice says, right beside me, making me jump out of my skin. Well...it *would* have...if, you know...Anyway, the Voice asks me, "Are you ready now?"

"No," I say. "I was just wondering: Was that me?"

The Voice knows what I'm talking about. "Yes to the lightbulb," the Voice tells me. "No to the wallet. You have to really concentrate to get the physical world to react, and in the meantime, things like simple human clumsiness come into play."

"Concentrate?" I repeat. I'm thinking that it never even occurred to me to want that bulb to explode.

And the Voice knows that, too. "You were *intense*," the Voice tells me, "but *unfocused*."

I consider this for a few seconds. "You mean if I concentrate on blowing up DeMarco's head..." I see that DeMarco has made it to the edge of the crowd and is starting to walk down the street.

"Nice try," the Voice says. "But that's not allowed."

"Hmmm," I say. "Thanks, anyway." And I start to follow DeMarco.

I'm running after DeMarco, who's crossed Broad Street, and just as I get to the corner, there're suddenly so many cars it looks like there's a direct line from Detroit, where they make them, right past this street corner. So there I am, bouncing in frustration, waiting for a break in the traffic, when it suddenly occurs to me: *Hey, I'm dead. If I want to cross against traffic, who's going to know or care?*

I'm about to step off the curb when someone says, "Hey. Little boy. How come your feet don't touch the ground?"

I turn, real slow, like maybe there could be some other kid around who's not quite substantial enough to stay on the sidewalk.

The speaker is this little old lady, dressed all in black the way little old ladies do, and—sure enough—she's looking right at me. She's with a younger woman who asks her, "What're you talking about, Ma?"

"That boy"—her finger is shaky, but, except for its movement, it's pointed at me—"his feet don't reach all the way to the ground." To me, she demands, "How come?"

"Aw, Ma," the younger one complains.

But the older one is waiting for an answer, so I say, trying to think of something reasonable but not scary, "Ahm...New shoes."

The woman slaps her hand to her forehead. "Such a mouth! In my day, children knew how to talk to their elders with respect."

"I'm talking to you with respect," the daughter objects. "Whaddya want, Ma? I thought you said you didn't feel good. I thought you said you wanted to go home. I'm taking you home, ain't I?"

The traffic finally slows down, and I figure I'd better cross now or risk losing DeMarco, but the woman who can see me is saying, "Yeah, yeah, my old heart has to give out sometime, why not now?"

"Ma, you been saying that for fifteen years now," the daughter says.

But the mother says, "Oh, my," and she sinks to the pavement, except that I can clearly see her still standing.

I feel the presence of the Voice. The Voice says, "Welcome home, Maria."

"Well!" the old woman tells the Voice. "It's about time! I'm eighty-two years old and I been waiting for you near half of that time. What took you so long?"

Her daughter, meanwhile, is screaming for help, on her knees, loosening her mother's collar to give her more air—though you know with the old lady's type, they don't like *any* skin to show—and all the while the daughter doesn't even realize that her mother is dead already.

The woman, Maria, reaches down and caresses her daughter's cheek. "Such a fuss," she says. "No need to make a scene. You were a good daughter, though I was seventeen hours in labor with you."

For a moment the daughter pauses in her frantic attempts to revive the old woman, and her own hand goes to the cheek her mother has touched. But then she begins hollering again.

"Headstrong, too," Maria says, but I don't know which of us she's talking to—me, her daughter, or the Voice.

"How come she could see me?" I ask the Voice.

"Sometimes," the Voice explains, "the dead can be seen by the almost dead."

"Ha!" Maria crows. "I knew it wasn't no damn shoes," and to the Voice she says, "Come on," and she hustles the Voice down that path that is like raspberry ripple ice cream.

I take off in the direction I last saw DeMarco.

But by this time he's nowhere in sight.

I pause and consider: For someone who can detonate street lamps without lifting a finger, finding a scum like DeMarco shouldn't be all that hard. I picture DeMarco in my mind, and I become aware of a path I hadn't noticed before—one that's like stroking a piece of velvet against the nap. So I follow that, and I end up at a two-story walk-up. Just by concentrating on following the path, I float up into the air and through the closed door.

Sure enough, it's DeMarco's apartment. There he is, sitting at the kitchen table, counting out the money I collected.

Apparently DeMarco doesn't live alone—he has a dog: It's big and it's ugly, and it immediately jumps to its feet, its claws skittering on the yellowed linoleum. It lunges at me, barking like crazy.

I take an instinctive step backward, which brings me through the closed door and back out onto the landing, and I hear a thud and a startled *yip* as the dog tries to follow.

"What is it, boy?" DeMarco says. The legs of his chair scrape against the floor. "Who's out there?" he yells through the door.

Not me—not *out there*—I've remembered that I no longer need to worry about minor inconveniences like being ripped apart by vicious dogs, and I've stepped back into the room.

The dog goes crazy, barking again, and he lunges again. This time I stand my ground. Same result, though: After the dog passes through me, once more he crashes into the door. Just so as not to confuse DeMarco, to let him know that there isn't anyone lurking on the landing, I step away from the door and into the room.

The dog attacks again—and smacks into the back of the couch.

"Aw, you stupid mutt," I tell him, "you're just the kind of stupid mutt that gets run over,"- 'cause if I figure if the thing can see me, then it must be about to die.

But the Voice comes out of nowhere (I swear, I think the Voice enjoys sneaking up on me to see me jump) and says, "Actually, some of the living are more sensitive to the dead than others—most animals, certain very young children, and a few adults can sense you."

"No kidding?" I say, not—to be honest—especially relieved to hear the dog's lifespan is not in jeopardy.

But maybe the dog isn't as stupid as it looks, because it gives up on trying to sink its teeth into me and just jumps up and down in front of me. I keep moving, and DeMarco, of course, has no idea what's going on.

"What're you doing, you dumb dog?" he demands. He opens the apartment door, just to make sure there's no one out there, and meanwhile I race the dog around the kitchen table. The mutt goes skidding on the floor and crashing into the chairs. This dog's a *long* way from its graceful wolf ancestors, and—in the tight circle we're making around the little table—his back half has trouble going in the same direction as his front half. So I make things easier for him: I jump onto the table itself. The dog follows, then goes sliding right off the far end, taking with it the money DeMarco was counting and the bowl of soup he'd had cooling. Minestrone, and by the smell of it, not half bad.

The dog is yapping, DeMarco is yelling at the dog, and whoever lives downstairs is banging a broom handle on the ceiling and hollering at both of them.

DeMarco grabs hold of the dog's collar, and he smacks it on the snout with a rolled-up magazine.

I stop egging the dog on, 'cause I don't want it to get

beaten on my behalf—even if it is dumb and ugly and eager to get a taste of me.

The dog sits down sulkily, then decides to make the best of things and begins lapping up that spilled mine-strone soup. It keeps an eye on me, though, and occasionally gives a throaty growl.

"All right, all right," DeMarco yells down at the neighbor who's still banging away on the ceiling. "Give it a rest already."

I notice that he picks up the money before he goes after the bowl and spoon. He doesn't wipe up the spill, leaving that to the dog. He just ladles a bit more soup from the pot into the bowl. Then he sits down to resume counting the money.

I concentrate on the bulb hanging over the table.

It explodes, showering tiny slivers of glass onto De-Marco, who jumps to his feet yelling, "What the hell?"

The dog, of course, guesses I'm responsible, and—since the soup is mostly gone, anyway—it takes to barking its fool head off at me.

"Shaddup!" DeMarco commands the dog. He looks up at what's left of the bulb in its socket. He brushes off his shoulders, tells himself, "Humph!" pushes his bowl of soup out of the way—to remind himself not to eat it since it's probably got glass in it—and turns once again to the money.

I think about that soup in that bowl getting hot. Getting really, really hot.

With a burst of smell of beef stock and the Parmesan he's sprinkled on top, the soup boils over the sides of the bowl.

DeMarco grabs the money out of the way of the soup that's still bubbling, even as it spreads across the table, and he hurriedly stands before it reaches the end of the table and begins dripping onto the floor.

The dog gives a sharp bark at DeMarco's sudden movement, but it's not interested in any more soup.

DeMarco goes "Humph!" again, though this time he sounds less ticked off and more worried.

Apparently deciding the kitchen is out to get him, DeMarco goes into the living room and sits on the couch, where he piles the money on the cushion to count out.

I concentrate on the faded throw pillow next to him.

It falls to the floor.

The dog barks because it can't figure how I moved the pillow without touching it. DeMarco figures the dog has knocked it down with its sniffing, so he ignores it.

So I cause it to blow up.

Feathers shoot into the air, then settle, like a major incident at a chicken coop. The dog goes chasing after feathers, baying like a bloodhound on the trail of something good.

DeMarco backs away from the couch *and* the money.

He goes into the bathroom, and I figure if he's going to do anything disgusting, I'm outta there, but all he wants is to wash his face.

I can see myself in the mirror over the sink, but I don't think anything of that, since all along I've been able to see my own arms and legs—not to mention Stewart and Maria. But then DeMarco, straightening, reaching for a towel, looks into the mirror, too.

"Holy—" he sputters. "Johnny! You *are* alive!" He tries to sound pleased. "I was sure—" But then he turns around and, of course, there's no sign of me. He turns back to the mirror.

I wave at him.

He spins to see if he can maybe catch me ducking somewhere to hide.

I wave again, though he can't see that until he faces the mirror again. I make the bathroom light explode.

DeMarco eases out of the bathroom.

There's a picture on the wall of some bridge, probably in Italy—I figure it must have come with the apartment, 'cause I can't see DeMarco spending money on art, except maybe the kind that comes on a calendar. But in any case, I tip it on the wall as he passes. Then I send a chair toppling to the floor.

"What is it?" DeMarco says. "What do you want?"

I, of course, cannot answer.

"I'm not the one who killed you," he tells me.

No kidding. Does he think being dead has damaged my brain? I cause the money I collected, bills and change, to rise up off the couch cushion.

"*What?*" DeMarco demands.

I throw a quarter at him, bouncing it off his forehead, which is better aim than I ever had when I was alive.

"Oh," he says. "The money. Sure, sure; the money. Take it. I was just going to bring it to your mother. Honest. I was just trying to count it for her."

Liar. I *saw* the envelope that was going to my mother.

I throw another coin at him—a nickel this time—but he sees it coming and ducks.

"Take it!" he tells me.

The dog barks once, sharply, as though to repeat what DeMarco is saying.

DeMarco has a radio on a stand next to the couch. I make it turn on full blast, then start to rock it back and forth.

The downstairs neighbor complains with the broom handle again.

"Jeez!" DeMarco says, rushing forward to steady the radio. "Whaddya want? You want *me* to bring the money to your mother?"

I stop rocking the radio.

"All right, all right," he says. "How about if I bring it now?" He scoops my twenty-dollar bill off the couch.

With my mind I pick up the two coins I threw at him, and I bounce them off the back of his head.

"All right, already," he tells me.

The dog barks again.

"Shaddup," DeMarco tells it, "you useless mongrel."

While he's bending to turn down the volume of the radio, and while the dog is watching him, I sneak up behind the dog and yell, "Boo!"

Startled, the dog nips DeMarco on the rear end, for which I decide maybe I like the miserable mutt after all.

So that's it. Naturally I don't trust DeMarco farther than I can see him, so I go with him to my mother's, even though that's the last place I want to be. But it's worse even than I thought, because she hasn't heard yet—he's the one who has to break the news to her about what happened. I wish then that I hadn't been so efficient with haunting DeMarco, because it would have been better if someone else told her first. Nobody should get news like that from a scum like DeMarco.

Although my mother is usually pretty quick, this news seems to slow her wits. At first she asks if DeMarco is talking about my father—though there's no way DeMarco could have word of my father in Ireland. Then she insists he's mistaken: It's another boy who has been killed, or maybe it's me—but I've only been hurt.

DeMarco tries to act all somber and bighearted—is there *anything* more repulsive than a scum who tries to act respectable?—and he hands her the money without a hint of explanation of how he has come to decide to bring it to her.

My mother just stares at the envelope with the money in it.

DeMarco is obviously disappointed that she doesn't even look to see how much is in there—*I'm* disappointed that she doesn't even look to see how much is in there. I wonder whether I should do some little thing to let her know I'm there, but I doubt that blowing up her couch cushions would be a real comfort to her at this time. She just says, "Thank you for letting me know," and then she asks him to leave.

I can tell this is exactly what DeMarco has been waiting to hear. He's through that door faster than Stewart came through the window. I'm tempted to leave with him, 'cause I can tell my mother doesn't want to cry in front of him, and I know she'd never have wanted to cry in front of me, either, but I can't just abandon her like this.

She drops the money onto the kitchen table, still without looking at it. I know it won't make her feel better, but it will make things easier later. I follow her into my little sister's room. Rosie is still young enough that sometimes she needs to take a nap, especially after a hard morning of playing with her dolls. My mother stands for a moment in the doorway, then moves into the room. She leans in close to Rosie, and suddenly I realize what she's doing.

I remember when Rosie was a baby and my father was still with us. He used to tease my mother because of how she worried about everything, how she would look in on Rosie when she was sleeping, to make sure that Rosie was all right, that she was still breathing. "She used to poke you, too," he told me, "if you were sleeping too quietly." We'd all laugh—my mother, too—at how she was willing to risk waking us for the assurance that all was right with us. My mother laughed, but she continued to check Rosie's breathing.

Now my mother crouches beside Rosie's bed, but she doesn't need to poke her: Rosie's little chest is moving up and down. All is right with one of my mother's children

Without a sound, my mother begins rocking back and forth on her heels.

I remember what the Voice said about very young children being able to see me, and I wonder if Rosie would be able to see me—if she could pass a message on to my mother for me. But I don't want to wait for Rosie to wake up. I want to comfort my mother *now*, and I don't know how. All I know how to do is throw things and make things explode. I know that no matter how loudly I shout, she won't be able to hear me.

But then I remember the old woman, Maria, and how she caressed her daughter's cheek, and for a moment the daughter almost knew she was there.

Instead of shouting, I whisper.

What I whisper is this: "Don't be sad."

My mother stops rocking. Although she doesn't look up, I believe she's listening.

I have nothing to say and I have everything to say. I whisper, "Don't be sad." And because I've been thinking about my father who abandoned us, I add, "Don't be angry. I'm sorry I had to leave, but everything will be all right." I *think* everything will be all right. Everything being all right is a path I can sense, like daisies on a hot summer day. I finish, "Meanwhile, it's time to let go, and to move on."

Can she hear me? I can't be sure. But she puts her hand to her lips and she blows a kiss, not at the still-sleeping Rosie, but up into the air.

Letting go and moving on strikes me as good advice. It's such good advice that I decide to take it myself.

Without a backward glance, I call out to the Voice, "I'm ready."

Vivian Vande Velde is the author of many books, ranging from picture books for the very young to fantasy novels for adults. Her novels for younger readers include the medieval mystery comedy *Never Trust a Dead Man*, which was named a *School Library Journal* Best Book of the Year, won an Edgar Award from the Mystery Writers of America, and was an ALA Best Book for Young Adults; *Magic Can Be Murder*, an IRA Children's Choice; *There's a Dead Person Following My Sister Around* and *Tales from the Brothers Grimm and the Sisters Weird*, both IRA Young Adults' Choices; as well as *Companions of the Night*, *Dragon's Bait*, and *User Unfriendly*, all available in Harcourt editions. A native of New York state, Ms. Vande Velde lives with her family in Rochester.

SCIENCE
in a Bottle

SCIENCE

in a Bottle

by Sandra Markle

Illustrated by June Otani

SCHOLASTIC INC.
New York Toronto London Auckland Sydney
Mexico City New Delhi Hong Kong

24 23 22 21 20 19   11 12 13 14 15 16/0

Printed in the U.S.A.   40

First Scholastic printing, revised edition, December 1999

Contents

Before You Start... 6

Can You Pick Up a Bottle Without Touching It? ...10

It's a Gas..13

What's Inside the Empty Bottle? 17

Test Your Lung Power 19

Perform Bottle Magic and Fool Your Friends 23

Magnify It..26

Make Your Own Thermos 29

Make Liquid Art...33

Make a Fountain in a Bottle............................36

Make a Bottle Flowerpot................................43

Make an Amazing Water-Producing Box 48

Raise Sea Monkeys.......................................53

Before You Start

Can you pick up a bottle without
    touching it?
Can you make a fountain in a bottle?
Can you prove that an empty bottle
    isn't empty?
Can you raise "sea monkeys" in a
    bottle?

Yes, you can do all this and more! All you
need are some materials you will find at home
or can buy cheaply at a grocery, gardening
store, aquarium supply store, or hardware
store. Then do the activities in this book.

You'll discover science can help you do some exciting things.

You'll be using plastic and glass bottles of different sizes in all of the activities.

You don't have to buy any bottles — just recycle. Collect used containers. Peel off the labels. Have an adult remove any plastic ring left by a twist-off cap. Then wash the bottles out and set them in a dish drainer in the sink — upside down with the caps off — to dry.

Any bottles that you don't cut up you can also wash and use again. That way you can enjoy investigating and help the earth, too.

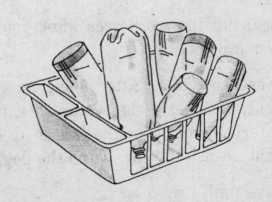

Remember

- Make sure you have all the materials you need before you start.

- Be careful using scissors and other tools.

- Clean up the work area after you finish your project.

- Conserve water. After doing an experiment, transfer clean water to a pail or watering can. Use the water to water plants, wash the car, bathe the dog, etc.

- Have fun!

Some Things You'll Need

Can You Pick Up a Bottle Without Touching It?

Does this sound like a magic trick? With a little science, you can do it two different ways and amaze your friends.

You'll need:

A 16-ounce plastic soft drink bottle
A plastic straw
A balloon

First, bend the straw about a third of the way from one end. Keep the straw bent while you slide it through the neck of the bottle.

Once inside the bottle, the straw will straighten slightly. Pull it up slowly until the hook formed by the bend touches both sides of the bottle. Continue to pull slowly and you'll have just enough of a connection to the bottle to lift it.

Now use the balloon to lift the bottle. Does that seem impossible? But you can do it — by adding air!

Insert the round balloon inside the bottle. Stretch the neck of the balloon out through the bottle top and blow into it. As soon as the balloon swells enough to press against both sides of the bottle, pinch the neck shut. Then lift the bottle.

Easy!

It's a Gas

What gives a soft drink its fizz? The answer is bubbles of carbon dioxide gas. The carbon dioxide gas is added to the soft drink solution before it's bottled. But if you've ever taken a sip of a soft drink that has gone flat, you know that something happens to this gas after the bottle is opened. Does it escape into the air? Try this experiment to find out.

You'll need:

3 identical 16-ounce bottles of a soft drink
3 balloons with mouths big enough to fit
    the neck of the bottles
A large bowl
A drinking glass

Put one soft drink in the refrigerator and leave the other two at room temperature overnight.

The next day, take the cap off one of the room temperature bottles. As soon as you take the cap off, pour a little of the soft drink into a glass. See all the bubbles rising to the surface and bursting? That's carbon dioxide at work.

Now quickly slip a balloon over the neck of the bottle. Slide it down far enough to cover the screw top ridges. Wait fifteen minutes. The balloon will puff up as it traps the escaping carbon dioxide gas.

Now use the other two bottles of soft drink to try another experiment. This time you'll find out whether or not chilling the soft drink will help it keep its fizz longer.

First, get the room temperature bottle and set it in a bowl full of hot water. Then take the cold bottle out of the refrigerator. Quickly take the caps off both bottles, cover the tops with balloons, and return the cold bottle to the refrigerator.

Wait fifteen minutes.

To check which bottle lost the most carbon dioxide gas, look at the balloons. The bigger the balloon, the more carbon dioxide was trapped.

COLD BOTTLE   WARM BOTTLE

Put the chilled bottle back in the refrigerator and replace the hot water in the bowl. Wait another fifteen minutes, then compare the balloons one more time.

If you were taking bottles of a soft drink along on a picnic, do you think it would be worthwhile to try to keep opened bottles chilled?

What's Inside the Empty Bottle?

The bottle may look empty — but it's not. It's full of air, as you will see when you do this activity.

You'll need:

A 2-liter plastic soft drink bottle
A balloon with a neck big enough to
    fit over the bottle's mouth
A large saucepan
A mixing bowl

Put the bowl in the sink and fill it with hot water. Fill the saucepan half full of cold water and set it on the counter close to the sink.

Slip the neck of the balloon over the top of the bottle. Set the bottle in the bowl of hot water. Hold the balloon steady.

The balloon will puff up as the heat makes the air molecules inside the bottle move apart. The more the air expands and rises, the more the balloon will puff up.

Now, quickly move the bottle to the pan of cold water. What happens to the balloon? What do you think is happening to the air inside the bottle?

Test Your Lung Power

Did you ever wonder how much air moves in and out of your lungs when you breathe? Is it a lot or only a little? Does it depend on how deep a breath you take?

Here's an activity that will let you find out.

You'll need:

A clear plastic 16-ounce soft drink or water
    bottle
A 2-gallon pail
A long flexible straw (the kind used in many
    portable drink bottles)
A permanent marker
A towel

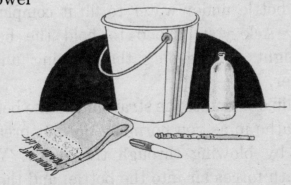

You may want to ask a friend to help you with this activity.

First fill the pail nearly full of water. Push the bottle under water to fill it completely full. Ask your friend to hold the bottle straight up, keeping the opening underwater.

Slip one end of the straw inside the bottle. Breathe in as you normally do, but breathe out by blowing through the straw. Your breath forces air into the bottle, and the air

will push out some of the water. That's why the water bubbles up around the bottle.

Lift the bottle out and dry one side. Mark the water level.

Dunk the bottle again and repeat the test. This time, though, take a *really* deep breath and force out all the air you can. Did you push out more water than the first time? A lot more or only a little more?

Human lungs can hold more than a gallon of air. The amount of air flowing in and out of your lungs is important. It's inside the lungs that your body takes in oxygen and gives off the waste gas carbon dioxide. Oxygen is carried by the blood throughout the body to the cells, the body's basic building blocks. There it is combined with food nutrients to produce the energy your body needs to grow and to be active.

Now, think about times when you breathe faster or draw fuller breaths, such as when you are playing hard or when you're afraid. Why do you think you move more air in and out of your lungs at those times?

Perform Bottle Magic and Fool Your Friends

Invite some friends over and trick them with a bit of science magic.

You'll need:

A 1-liter clear plastic soft drink bottle
A pushpin
Kitchen sink

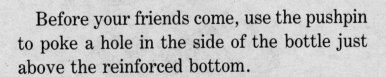

Before your friends come, use the pushpin to poke a hole in the side of the bottle just above the reinforced bottom.

Now you're ready to do the trick for your audience. Ask everyone to stand around the kitchen sink.

Fill the sink nearly full of water. Hold the bottle under the faucet to fill it completely full. Be careful not to squeeze the bottle, because water will squirt out the hole, and you don't want your friends to know about the hole.

Now hold your fingers over the bottle's mouth while you quickly dunk it underwater.

Next, turn the bottle so it's upside down. **Be sure your finger is now pressed over the tiny hole, sealing it.**

Lift the bottle slowly, showing your friends that the water does not run out of the bottle until the mouth is above the surface of the water and air can slip inside.

Plunge the bottle back underwater to show that this stops the water from pouring out.

Now, refill the bottle. Ask for a volunteer from the audience to try to start and stop the water flow just as you did.

Unless your friend happens to put a finger over the hole, the "trick" won't work. As long as air is able to slip in through the hole, water will pour out of the bottle even while its mouth is underwater.

Your friends will be stumped. How did *you* do it?

Of course, when air enters the bottle through the hole, it pushes water out and creates bubbles. If your friends see bubbles, your secret is out.

Magnify It

Is there something tiny you'd like to be able to see better? Science and a bottle can help you.

You'll need:

A 2-liter clear plastic bottle
A piece of newspaper

Fill the bottle nearly full of water and set it on a table or counter. Hold the newspaper close to one side of the bottle. Look at the print through the bottle. The print will appear bigger.

The reason the print appears enlarged is that light rays reflected off the paper are bent as they pass through the curved sides of the bottle and the water. This makes the image seem to be stretched by tricking your eyes into thinking that the light is coming from a bigger area.

A lens or magnifying glass works the same way — the more the lens is curved, the more it appears to stretch the object.

How else has the bottle magnifier changed the way the print looks? Move the printed page closer and farther away; up and down. Does this change the way the print looks? Now look at a picture instead of words. In what ways does the bottle magnifier change the way the picture looks?

Now use your bottle magnifier to look at different objects, such as your finger . . . a penny . . . a strand of your hair and a hair from your cat or dog . . . a feather . . . a stamp. What do you see that you couldn't see before?

Make Your Own Thermos

Need to keep soup hot or a soft drink cold? A thermos can do both. Do you wonder why it's so good at keeping temperatures from changing? Make your own thermos and find out.

You'll need:

A large glass or plastic jar with wide mouth and lid (such as a pickle container)
A 12-inch square of corrugated cardboard (from a box)
2 identical cans or bottles of juice, 6 ounces or less
Scissors
Aluminum foil
An old newspaper

Chill the juice containers for at least an hour.

Cut the cardboard into squares that will fit through the mouth of the jar. Stack these up on the bottom of the jar.

Next, wrap one juice container in three layers of aluminum foil.

Place the wrapped container inside the jar on top of the cardboard. (Remove layers of cardboard as needed so the juice container is below the mouth of the jar.)

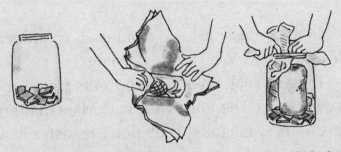

Crumple the newspaper and pack it tightly around the juice on all sides.

Tightly seal the lid of the jar. Set the other container of juice next to the sealed jar but without touching it.

After an hour, take the juice out of your homemade thermos. Take off the aluminum foil* and feel the outside of both juice containers. Which feels colder?

*Save the aluminum foil to use again or recycle.

Pour a glass of juice from each container. Taste them. Which tastes colder?

Like a real thermos, the one you made surrounded the juice with materials that are insulators, meaning they don't transfer heat energy easily.

Usually a thermos has double glass walls with a vacuum (a space containing absolutely nothing, not even air) between them. The glass walls are also silvered on the inner surface. Like a mirror, this shiny surface reflects the heat energy. The stopper is made of cork or plastic — materials that slow the transfer of heat.

Make Liquid Art

Pour a tablespoonful of vegetable oil into a glass of water. Did it surprise you to see that the oil floats on the surface of the water? Although many materials will dissolve in water, oil won't. And since it's less dense than water, the oil floats on top.

By adding oil to colored water, you can create a fluid, ever-changing work of art.

You'll need:

A small bottle with a tight cap (can be plastic
    or glass)
Clear vegetable oil
Red, yellow, or green food coloring
A teaspoonful of glitter
Colored beads, small scraps of colored plastic
    (such as bits of cut-up plastic bottles),
    small colorful buttons, or plastic toys

Fill the bottle half full of water and add
enough of one food color to make the water
a vivid hue.

Add enough oil to fill the bottle partway
up the neck.

Dump in the glitter and other items.

Screw the cap on tight.

To set your liquid art in motion, hold the neck in one hand and the base in the other and tip the bottle from side to side. Do this very slowly at first and then a little harder.

What happens to the items you added?

What happens to the water and oil as they move together?

Hold the bottle still and watch the changes that take place as the solution slows down. What else might you put into the bottle to add to this artistic show?

Make a Fountain in a Bottle

You don't notice the weight of the air pushing on you from all directions — but it does. You can do this demonstration to prove that air exerts pressure.

Fill a glass with water. Get an index card or a piece of cardboard that is slightly larger than the opening and place it over the glass. Hold the card in place with your fingertips while you turn the glass straight upsidedown. Then take your fingers away from the card.

Try this outdoors or over a sink because if you don't have the glass straight up and down, it won't work. If you do, the card will keep the water from rushing out. The secret is that the air pressure pushing up on the card exerts more force than the water does pushing down.

Now, use the force that air exerts to create a fountain inside a bottle.

You'll need:

2 clear plastic soft drink bottles (1-liter size)
Modeling clay
2 plastic straws
A pushpin (map tack)
Blue food coloring
Duct tape (optional)

First you need to punch holes in each straw using the pushpin. Start about an inch from the end of the straw. Punch about a dozen holes all the way around the straw. Make the holes in several rows. Wiggle the pin to enlarge the holes.

Next, shape a ball of clay about as big as the neck of the bottles. Press one straw against the side of this ball. Shape the clay so it surrounds the straw, *but be sure the clay does not cover the opening of the straw.* Also, be sure the holes in the straw are below the clay.

Now press the other straw
into the clay ball opposite the
first straw. Make it stick
straight up.

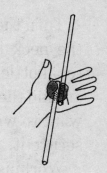

Fill one bottle three-quarters full of water.
Add enough coloring to make the water
bright blue. Put the clay cap onto the bottle
with the straw pointed straight down into
the water.

Turn the other bottle upside down, sliding the neck over the second straw. Push the top bottle into the clay. Press more clay around the bottles to seal the necks. You may want to wrap duct tape over the clay to help secure it.

Working at the kitchen sink, carefully turn the pair of bottles over so the one with water is on top. Watch what happens.

Gravity causes the water in the top bottle to drain into the bottom bottle. When the water level falls below the open end of the straw, though, water begins to spurt out the straw.

This happens because as the amount of water in the bottle goes down, the remaining air expands. The air pushes down on the remaining water. Some is forced into the small holes you made in the straw and up through the straw. When it reaches the top of the straw, it spurts out.

To keep on watching this action, turn the bottles over so the top bottle is the one full of water again.

How to Cut a Bottle in Two

For each of the next three activities you will need to cut apart a 2-liter plastic bottle. You need a ruler, a marker, and a pair of sharp scissors.

Here's what you do:

Measure as the directions tell you to do and make a mark on the side of the bottle. Then draw a line around the bottle at that mark.

Ask an adult to cut the top piece off along the line.

Then you're ready to do the activity.

(1) Poke a hole with the scissors.
(2) Cut along the line.

Make a Bottle Flowerpot

Usually when you water a plant, the water goes down through the soil to the base of the pot. Not with this flowerpot! The water goes from the base up through the soil. How does this happen? Do the activity and see.

You'll need:

A 2-liter soft drink bottle
  (label and cap removed)
A marker
A ruler
Scissors with sharp points
Potting soil
An old cotton tube sock
A small house plant,
   such as an African violet

First, you need to cut the bottle apart to make a pot for your plant. Measure about four inches down from the top and make a mark. Measure six inches up from the base and make another mark. (Follow the directions on page 42 for cutting the bottle.)

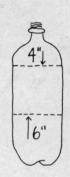

Next, cut a strip of the sock about three inches wide and eight inches long.

Turn the top piece of the bottle upside down. Push the cotton strip through the bottle neck so only about three inches remain in the top of the bottle.

Set this piece in the bottle's base. Spoon in enough potting soil to fill the top piece halfway.

Place your plant in the center and carefully add soil around it, completely covering the roots. Gently pat down the soil so it will help support the plant.

Finally, lift up the top piece and fill the base about half full of water. Push the cotton strip down into the water as you set the plant back onto the base.

To see what will be happening to your plant, fill a glass with water and add enough food coloring to turn it a bright hue. Then touch just the edge of a paper towel to the top of the colored water. As you watch, the water will slowly creep up the paper.

This happens because the water touching the paper moves up into the tiny spaces between the fibers. Because water molecules, the tiny building blocks of water, tend to stick together, more water moves up into the paper. This pushes the first water molecules higher, and slowly this process makes the water climb to the top of the paper towel.

Water moves through the cotton strip into the soil this same way. As the plant's roots take in water, the process continues to pull up water from the base. Just remember to add more water to the base once in a while and your plant will have just the amount of water it needs at all times.

Add a little fertilizer to the water from time to time to keep the plant supplied with the chemicals, such as nitrogen, that it needs to be healthy.

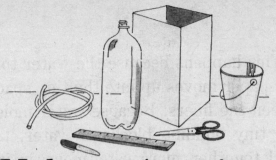

Make an Amazing Water-Producing Box

Do you believe a box can produce water? With the help of science, you can make your friends believe you've made one that does.

You'll need:

A 2-liter plastic bottle
Scissors with sharp points
A cardboard box deep enough to hide the
    bottle after its top is cut off
A ruler
A marker
2 feet of 1/2-inch flexible plastic tubing
    (available in stores that sell aquarium or
    garden supplies)
A plastic bucket
Blue food coloring (optional)

Ask an adult to cut the top off the bottle just below where it flares out. (See cutting directions on page 42.)

Make a hole in the side of the bottle two inches below the top. The hole should be big enough for the tubing to slide through easily.

Place the bottle inside the box. Mark the spot on the box that's directly opposite the hole in the bottle. Cut a matching hole in the box.

Slide the tube through the box and into the bottle inside the box. Make sure the end of the tube doesn't quite touch the bottom of the bottle.

Fill the bottle with water to just below the hole.

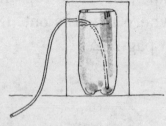

Place the box on a table with a plastic bucket or wastebasket under the end of the tube.

To be sure no one can look inside the box, close the lid or put an oversized piece of stiff cardboard on top.

Now get the top piece of the bottle. This piece will be used as a funnel. Place it with the neck down on the lid of the box and trace around the neck. Cut the circle out and fit the bottle neck into the hole.

You're ready to make magic! Tell your friends that you have a magic box that produces water. To get it started, pour water into the funnel just until water starts to flow out the tube. It won't take much additional water.

Once the water level inside the bottle is above the hole, it creates a siphon that keeps the water flowing.

Just for fun, measure exactly how much water you pour in the funnel. Then have a friend collect the water by cupfuls before dumping it to demonstrate how much *more* came out.

To make your magic water-producing box even more magical, add blue food coloring to the water in the reservoir.

To work, a siphon needs two things:

(1) The section of the tube that's extending down from the hole in the box must be longer than the part inside the bottle that goes up to the hole.

(2) There must be air pressure pushing down on the water inside the bottle so there's no break in the column of water flowing through the tube.

As long as these two conditions are met, the siphon will keep the water flowing until the reservoir has been drained.

Raise Sea Monkeys

"Sea monkey" is the nickname sometimes given to tiny brine shrimp. These little shrimp are among the few kinds of animals able to live in Utah's Great Salt Lake, where the water is, on the average, ten percent saltier than the oceans.

These lively critters are also easy to raise at home. Just start up a bottle aquarium and watch the action. Then try the experiment to learn even more about brine shrimp.

You'll need:

A 2-liter clear plastic bottle

A ruler

A marker

Scissors with sharp points

A spoon

Measuring spoons

Two tablespoons rock salt, or kosher salt

Brine shrimp eggs (inexpensive and available at pet shops that sell aquarium supplies because they're raised to feed tropical fish)

A magnifying glass

A package of dry yeast

Cut the top off the bottle about two inches below the neck. (See the directions on page 42.) Be sure the bottle is clean.

Fill the bottle nearly full of water and let it sit for a day. Add the rock salt and stir until it's completely dissolved. Sprinkle 1/4 teaspoon of brine shrimp eggs on the surface of the water. Place the bottle in a warm spot that isn't directly in the sun.

Over the next few days, watch for signs of movement in the bottle. The newly hatched shrimp will be very tiny, but you'll be able to see them swimming in a jerky up-and-down motion.

Feed the shrimp by sprinkling a few grains of powdered yeast on the water every third day.

Keep a journal of your observations. How many days did it take for the first eggs to hatch?

As the brine shrimp grow bigger, use your magnifying glass to look for eggs inside the females.

In what other ways do the females look different from the males? How long is it before you see new baby brine shrimp in the water?

You may want to do some more experiments to see what conditions affect how quickly brine shrimp eggs hatch.

Set up three bottles full of brine water just as you did before. Label these 1, 2, and 3.

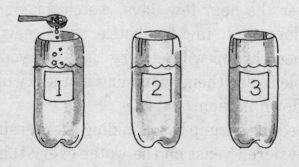

Add an extra tablespoonful of rock salt to bottle 1.

Set bottle 2 in a place that will stay cool.

Put bottle 3 in the dark. Check regularly for newly hatched brine shrimp. Did any hatch more quickly than in your original batch? Which was the slowest to hatch? Of course, you'll need to repeat this test two more times to be sure that the results you got are likely to happen every time.

Now, plan a test using ice and one using a flashlight to test how temperature and exposure to bright light affect brine shrimp behavior. Don't forget to repeat these tests, too. Record the results in your journal.

Fast Facts About Brine Shrimp

- Brine shrimp live throughout the world, wherever there is very salty water. In the Great Salt Lake, there are sometimes so many brine shrimp that they make the water appear red or brownish-red. This color is created by the green algae the brine shrimp eat. During the digestion process the algae turns red. Since the brine shrimp are nearly transparent, this color shows.

- Brine shrimp eggs are very hardy. They can withstand being baked by the sun or exposed to freezing winter temperatures and still hatch.

- The curator of the Steinhart Aquarium of the California Academy of Sciences was the first to discover that brine shrimp make good food for aquarium fishes. Besides being cheap and easy to raise, brine shrimp don't decay and pollute the tank if they aren't eaten immediately. Since the tiny shrimp are alive, they just keep on swimming around, providing in-between-meal snacks for hungry fish.